And then the words came naturally to her as he led her, line by line, step by step, through the scene... Carenza had done this scene with Nigel, a few days earlier. The stage directions had indicated that they kiss, and so they had. Carenza usually had no problems with kissing men on stage. It was not she herself, but the character, who did the kissing, who was tender, passionate, loving. It meant nothing.

But Gareth Llewellyn slid his hand under the heavy mass of her hair, at the nape of her neck, and drew her towards him with a world of tender authority in the gesture.

'"And this..."' She was youthful clay in his knowledgeable hands as he touched her lips very lightly with his. '"And this..."' his lips brushed her forehead like the caress of a silken scarf, '"...the greatest discords be."'

And on those words the voice deepened, the playfulness went out of his eyes to be replaced by intense and unstoppable desire. Her lips parted, her own eyes widened, and her mouth flowered under his... Only when he let her go, and she was Carenza Carlton again, did she start to shake.

'You shouldn't have done that!' she gasped. 'It was going a bit too far!'

*Another book you will enjoy*
*by LEE STAFFORD*

**LOVE TAKES OVER**

It wasn't exactly Trent Foxley-Castleford's fault that Laurel's adoptive father had sold their family business to Castleford Industries without consulting her—but she was still angry, and there was no way he was going to escape bearing the brunt of some of that anger...

# SHADOW IN THE WINGS

### BY

## LEE STAFFORD

**MILLS & BOON LIMITED**
ETON HOUSE   18-24 PARADISE ROAD
RICHMOND   SURREY   TW9 1SR

*First published in Great Britain 1991
by Mills & Boon Limited*

© Lee Stafford 1991

*Australian copyright 1991
Philippine copyright 1991
This edition 1991*

ISBN 0 263 77241 1

*Set in Times Roman 11 on 12 pt.
01-9109-51131 C*

*Made and printed in Great Britain*

# CHAPTER ONE

FROM a distance, as she walked along the deserted shore, it was possible only to discern that the girl was slender and long-legged in her blue jeans and sweater; that the wind that raced the white-capped waves up the beach whipped her long, soft brown hair about her face in unruly disorder.

As she drew closer, the man watching could see that her face was dreamy, with wide-curved lips and elongated eyes beneath fine, dark brows. She was exceptionally pleasing to look at, but, for all that, he regarded her sourly, wishing she would vanish and leave him to the solitude the stiff, chill wind and massing clouds drifting in from the sea ought to have guaranteed him.

But here she was, not only destroying his fragile peace with her presence, but, worse, she was actually talking to herself! Was she an escaped lunatic, perhaps?

Carenza, pacing the sand with her graceful, striding walk, was quite unaware of his irritated scrutiny. He sat all but immobile on an outcrop of rocks the incoming tide would submerge within the hour, and she was thinking herself deeply into the persona of a young sixteenth-century Venetian girl, speaking her words as she walked.

'... So that, dear lords, if I be left behind
    A moth of peace, and he go to the war,

The rites for why I love him are bereft me,
And I a heavy interim shall support
By his . . .'

Her voice trailed away as she bit her lip, seeking
the next line. The words were still new to her and
imperfectly learned; it would be a while until she
knew them well enough to lose herself in the character of the part. Annoyed with herself, she gazed
skywards, as if she would pluck the elusive phrase
from the darkening heavens.

'"By his dear absence. Let me go with him."'

The prompting voice spoke unwillingly, torn, despite its owner's desire to have nothing to do with
her or any other member of the human race, to
supply the missing words.

Carenza turned her head sharply, suddenly tossed
back into the present day. She had not seen him
until he spoke; had expected, on this capriciously
cold spring afternoon, to have the beach to herself.
She felt incredibly foolish, caught reciting aloud,
and he was looking at her as if the beach were his
private property, and she had no business being
there at all.

However, she had no intention of letting him see
her embarrassment, or of allowing his obvious displeasure to banish her. 'Thank you,' she said drily.

He inclined his head—ruffled, near-black hair,
tousled by the wind and just lightly touched with
grey at ears and temples. He had not moved from
his position, poised easily on the clump of rocks,
but there was a tensile, whipcord strength to his
body that made her think he might uncoil and
pounce at any moment, and a brooding disquiet

shadowed his dark, disapproving face. An angry humour lurked at the corners of his expressive mouth, and scathing, surprisingly light grey eyes, like rain-washed sky, raked her scornfully as he clapped his hands in slow, eloquently sarcastic applause.

'You have a long way to go with that, I think,' he remarked disparagingly.

Carenza folded her arms defensively and stared back at him, stung by his rudeness. 'I don't know the lines properly, as yet. I've only just started to learn them,' she said. 'Not that it's any of your business,' she could not resist adding tartly.

'My dear young woman, if you will speak lines aloud they become the property of anyone who happens to hear them,' he pointed out loftily. 'And think about what you're saying, while you're about it. You could put a bit more warmth into "the rites for why I love him", for example. What do you think Desdemona is talking about, for goodness' sake? Dusting the lounge? *Marital* rites—she wants to live with Othello as his wife, and make love.'

Carenza flushed uncomfortably. He was right, of course, but no one should talk this way to a newly met stranger.

'I hardly think——' she began primly.

He shrugged, and cut her off peremptorily. 'Then you should. *Othello* is a play about passion, jealousy and betrayal, about a Colossus of a man whose downfall is brought about because he's gulled into believing his wife in unfaithful,' he said.

Carenza gazed at him, puzzled and curious. His eyes were hard and ungiving, but his voice was soft with a respect that had nothing to do with her, and all to do with the work under discussion. And what a voice—quietly spoken, but hinting at an intensity of strength and feeling barely touched. Like a powerful, sophisticated engine, presently only ticking over. A Stradivarius of a voice, which rang bells deep in her consciousness, leaving her troubled because she did not know why.

'You are an expert on Shakespearian drama, then, I presume?' she asked, hiding her puzzlement behind a mask of scorn.

The shoulders rose and fell again, this time in a slight gesture of self-dismissal.

'Me? I'm an expert on nothing—except perhaps finding lonely Welsh beaches and endeavouring vainly to keep them to myself.'

'Sorry,' she said, with heavy sarcastic emphasis. 'Pardon me for existing! I've been walking on this particular beach over a period of years, as it happens, but I've never seen you before. I certainly wasn't aware that you had proprietorial rights! Do you live around here?'

'At the moment, I do.'

And now he stood up, lithe and taut and clearly intent on a swift exit. Suddenly and inexplicably, Carenza did not want him to go. He had been far from polite. Obviously he resented her presence, and wanted only his own company, but she was intrigued by her brief glimpse of his knowledge-ability, captivated by the musical resonance of his voice. As she had told him, she had been coming here for years, and thought she knew all the locals, at least by sight. He must be a newcomer, or she would surely have seen him before.

She fell into step beside him—he was anyhow walking in the same direction as she, towards the path which led from the beach. He ignored her completely, striding loosely along so that she was hard put to keep up with him, and she was piqued by his unsociability.

A little breathlessly, because she was walking quickly, she heard herself begin to prattle.

'Maybe I didn't sound too good, but I've only just started to read the part. We've scarcely even rehearsed, yet. But it's...it's odd that you should know it. Not one person in a million could have finished that line as you did.'

He slowed, then came to an abrupt halt; instinctively she stopped in her tracks, too, pinned to the spot by his irritated frown and the evident displeasure in the grey eyes.

'Look...' he said, and then sighed with heavily tried patience. 'I assume you are not a professional actress.'

It wasn't a question, and Carenza's lips parted in a faint, regretful smile.

'It shows that much? No, I belong to an amateur dramatic society. I suppose you are going to say that you think we've bitten off more than we can chew?'

Was that just a reflection of a smile curling around the hard, almost bitter line of his mouth?

'It really has nothing to do with me, has it?' he said firmly, stating his utter lack of interest in her, her dramatic aspirations, or anything else about her. 'But since you ask—well, yes, one could say you've been a touch ambitious. *Othello* is a masterpiece, and a complex and difficult work. You'd have done better to stick to something lighter, like *Lady Windermere's Fan*. Or what about *The Importance of Being Earnest*?'

Her laughter pealed out, irresistible and unexpected.

'We've done that!' She peered intently at him, with the charming shortsightedness she had adopted so successfully as Gwendolen, and thought he caught his breath swiftly, as if something had touched him. Then the hard mask descended once again.

'You have? Too bad. Well, that's my opinion, for what it's worth,' he said brutally. 'I wish you the best of luck.'

He turned and resumed his stride, without a word, and Carenza, determined not to intrude any further where she was so plainly not wanted, stood and watched him until he reached the point where the path divided. He took the right fork, as she had expected him to, because the left one led up to the farm, where she was heading. Then he turned the corner and was gone.

She shrugged, and, making a firm decision to dismiss the rude, annoying stranger from her mind, she continued on her way up to the weathered grey stone farmhouse with its jumble of roof-tops at varying levels, chimneys and outbuildings, that belonged to Dai and Bronwen Pritchard.

It was late afternoon, and Dai and his eldest son, Trefor, were bringing the cows up from the fields for milking, aided and abetted by Samantha, Carenza's fourteen-year-old sister, who was always known, by her own choice, as 'Sam' or 'Sammy'.

Sammy wore a pair of disreputable jeans, ripped at the knees, an enormous floppy sweater, two sizes too big, and muddy wellies. Her hair, several shades lighter brown than Carenza's, a colour she herself called with cheerful disparagement 'mucky straw', was tied back at the nape of her neck by an old checked scarf, and she carried a thin stick for chivvying reluctant animals on their way. Carenza smiled with rueful affection, thinking that her young sister looked as much a part of the scenery as any of the Pritchards.

'Hold the gate open properly, Sam, you twit,' Trefor called, with the lofty authority of his sixteen years.

'Who are you calling a twit, boyo?' she laughed back, swinging on the gate as she opened it to let the herd of black and white Herefords amble through and across the yard to the milking shed.

Not for the first time, Carenza said a silent prayer of thanks for Bronwen and Dai, this remote, peaceful outpost on the Welsh island of Anglesey, and for her old college mate, Fran, now living in California, who let Carenza make use of the caravan she kept in Dai's field. Where would she and Sammy have been, over the last few years, without this blessed bolt-hole? she wondered thankfully. For Sam, even more than for herself, it was home from home.

She had come here first as an eighteen-year-old drama student, after her mother had died leaving her alone in the world with a sister ten years her junior.

'You need some space,' Fran had said with practical sympathy, worried by Carenza's taut, strung-out nervousness, her apprehension about the future. 'I know just the place you can find it.'

So Carenza had spent most of the summer vacation there with Sammy, calmed by Dai's and Bronwen's unsentimental cheerfulness, their soft, lilting Welsh voices, the soothing closeness to nature and the absence of rush and bustle. She had done a lot of thinking, that summer. Sammy had been terrified of being split up from her sister and put into care, and Carenza knew she would have her work cut out to convince the authorities that she could maintain a home for them both. She had taken the only course possible for her. Abandoning the precarious prospect of an acting career, which had always been her dream, she had opted for teacher training and a secure future.

She and Sammy had succeeded in staying together, but at the price of Carenza's own ambitions. She had allowed herself to waste no time in regrets for the decision she could not have avoided. No way could she have let her little sister go to strangers. Even so, it had been a hard struggle, but eventually she had finished college and taken a job teaching English at a comprehensive school in the Midlands town where they lived. They had a tiny but practical two-bedroomed flat, and she ran a small car. She enjoyed her job, and put her utmost into it, but the life of her dreams carried on after work with the Spotlight Players, the dramatic society of which she was an enthusiastic member.

Carenza stood where she was until the cows passed by—there was little sense competing with fifty large Herefords intent on reaching the milking stalls—and then she crossed the yard and popped her head round the door of Bronwen's large but cluttered kitchen.

'Hi—are you busy?'

Bronwen, small and dark with the face of an animated pixie, brushed flour off the end of her nose, and grinned.

'Not so busy that I couldn't do a cuppa,' she said, reaching for the kettle. 'Dinner's on, but it'll be a while until they come in from milking.'

Carenza perched on a stool. Over the years she had used Fran's caravan, for all she had become good friends with Dai and Bronwen, she had always been careful not to impinge upon their busy, working life. They, in turn, had given her and Sammy the space they needed to be a family. Sometimes Bronwen invited them for a meal at the farmhouse, chats over cups of tea were frequent, and Sammy involved herself fully in helping out with jobs around the farm. It worked out admirably, and, without having intended to do so, Carenza found herself immediately drawn to ask Bronwen for information about the stranger on the beach, forgetting her decision to put the disturbing encounter right out of her mind.

'Do you know if there are any newcomers living round about?' she enquired as casually as possible, sipping tea from an enormous earthenware mug.

'Newcomers? Here?' Bronwen laughed. 'The same people have farmed the same land for as long as I can remember. There are always summer visitors, of course, but no permanent families have moved here, so far as I know.'

'And you'd know, if anyone did,' Carenza grinned, pushing back a strand of her soft, heavy brown hair. Bronwen was a reliable mine of local gossip. 'Only—there was this man on the beach whom I've never seen before.'

Bronwen raised a suggestive eyebrow. 'Go on. Sounds interesting, so far,' she said.

Carenza fended off the implication. The one bone of contention between Bronwen and herself was that the former thought that she should be—if not married—at least involved in a serious relationship. She could not understand why Carenza avoided her matchmaking intentions as she might have done the plague.

'That's not what I meant,' she said hastily. 'Honestly, Bronwen, you think of all men as husband-fodder! As a matter of fact, this one was rather a bad-tempered specimen. He wanted the entire beach to himself, and looked as if he would have liked to kill me for daring to invade his privacy.'

Bronwen cocked a curious ear. 'What was he like?'

'Like? Oh...' Carenza paused thoughtfully. 'Lean, dark, dramatic. Black hair. Profile like an Arab corsair and eyes like a predatory hawk. Amazing voice——'

'It certainly doesn't sound as if you missed much!' Bronwen exclaimed, smiling at Carenza's extravagant description. 'Someone like that ought to be instantly recognisable, especially in a small farming community like this! And, now you mention it, although I haven't met him, it might be Rhys Llewellyn's nephew.'

'You mean the old gentleman who owned the big house...what's it called...? Plas Gwyn, over towards Valley?' Carenza asked. 'I thought he died some time last summer . . . not that anyone ever saw much of him.'

'So he did, and left the house, which has belonged in his family for generations, to his nephew, having no children of his own,' Bronwen explained. 'Of course, you haven't been down often, over the winter, have you? Rhys's nephew . . . I can't recall his name . . . moved in, and by all accounts is even more reclusive than his uncle was. He's young—about thirty-six—but he lives alone, doesn't mix, or encourage callers. You're honoured if you got more than the time of day from him!'

'Oh, I got more than that!' Carenza said ruefully. 'And, believe me, it wasn't pleasant! If I see him again, I'll keep going in the opposite direction.'

But would she really? Lying in bed in the caravan that night, what came back to her was not so much the lean, arrogant, disapproving face, or the strange, light grey eyes, arresting as they were. What haunted her, spoke to her in the darkness, was that low, mellifluous, beautifully expressive voice. Where and when had she heard it before . . . or had it been only in dreams?

The caravan was pleasantly spacious for two people, one of whom spent most of her waking hours outdoors, Carenza reflected, sipping the morning tea thrust at her by Sammy before she went out to help with the early milking.

Sammy, who back home at the flat in Longbridge would lie in bed until lunchtime if she didn't have school, aimlessly wired up to her personal stereo and gazing vapidly at the ceiling, was up and out by daybreak on Anglesey, whatever the weather.

And this morning had broken fresh and sunny after yesterday's near-gale-force wind and dark skies.

Carenza stood with her hands clasped around her mug, gazing out through the large picture windows of the living area. The beach where she had walked yesterday was the nearest stretch of proper sandy shore to the farm, and even in high summer it never got very busy, because it was only accessible by little, winding, secretive lanes, away from the main roads around the island.

But Dai's field and the farmhouse looked out on a different aspect. The other side of a low wall was a small, shingly bay surrounded by rocks and pools which filled with seaweed and fishy creatures after every tide. Across a wide expanse of water, looking very close but actually only to be reached by several miles' drive around the bay and through Valley, the grey bulk of Holyhead mountain, with the town nestling at its base, reared into the pale blue morning sky. The windows of its houses winked as they caught the sun, whose rays danced on the sparkling water not more than a hundred yards from where she stood.

Carenza had an irresistible urge to be outside. Slipping into jeans and a sweatshirt, she closed the caravan door behind her and set off across the dew-damp grass towards the bay. Seagulls screamed fiercely overhead as she climbed the stile over the wall and jumped down on to the shingle, savouring the tangy marine scent of seaweed and salt water.

Her trainer-clad feet scrunched on the pebbles, and, unbidden, she heard *his* voice again, but this time not objecting irritably to her unwanted presence, or criticising her unpractised rendition of

Desdemona's speech. The voice she heard now came
to her from long ago, from her all too brief days
as a drama student, and a visit to the theatre their
class tutor had thought would be exemplary.

The play on that occasion had been *Henry V*,
and, although six years had elapsed, she remembered that visit now as clearly as if it had been
yesterday.

She even recalled sitting in the pub with a group
of her fellow students afterwards, and one of them
saying dejectedly, 'I don't know whether to be inspired or depressed. It's stupendous to know that
anyone can give so much to a performance, but it
only brings it home to you that you'll never be *that*
good, however hard you work!'

She remembered the clash of axe on shield, and
all the emotions evoked by the play. The loneliness
of kingship, the sway of rival dynasties on the
scarlet field of history, and one man's voice bringing
it all back to her in Henry's ringing St Crispin's
day address to his men before the battle of
Agincourt.

'We few, we happy few, we band of brothers;
For he today that sheds his blood with me
Shall be my brother...'

Carenza came to an abrupt, unplanned halt and
struck her forehead with her fist in exasperation
with her own stupidity. He had looked different
then, dressed in the garb of medieval England, his
black hair as yet untouched by grey, but his taut,
athletic body was unchanged, and it was no wonder
his voice had plagued her dreams.

'Rhys Llewellyn's nephew... I can't recall his name,' Bronwen, to whom theatrical matters meant little, had said vaguely. But Carenza was sure, now, beyond doubt that the man she had met yesterday on the beach had to be Gareth Llewellyn, reputedly one of the greatest exponents of Shakespearian drama the century had produced. It all fitted...the name, the looks, and, most of all, the voice.

She groaned aloud with astonishment and renewed embarrassment. This great actor-director had been obliged to listen to her pathetic attempts at Desdemona! No wonder his cold, patrician face had worn an expression of faintly amused disdain!

And worse—she had more or less told him that he had no idea what he was talking about! If only she had known, had realised in time! Certainly, if she saw him again—which was unlikely, according to Bronwen—she would keep well out of his way. It was humiliating enough to know that he must have been secretly laughing up his sleeve at her feeble efforts.

Her discovery had cast a cloud over Carenza's morning. She went back to the caravan and concentrated on frying bacon and eggs ready for when Sammy came back, ravenous as always, but she could not put it out of her mind.

It wasn't only the fact that she had been caught looking rather foolish. She could have lived with that, especially when the person who had witnessed it was someone she wasn't likely to encounter often—if at all.

But seeing Gareth Llewellyn, hearing him, thinking about him, had awoken old dreams, old ambitions she had thought to have buried fathoms deep under the superstructure of her calm, practical present-day life. She had been a promising drama student. She knew, without vanity, that she had potential, if it could only have been properly developed. Even now, sometimes, when she was on stage with the Spotlight Players, she felt the power surge through her veins, and knew it had never really left her.

But all that was part of another life, a life which she had never had the chance to live. She would never tread the stage with the likes of Gareth Llewellyn. She would never even know if she might, perhaps, have been good enough to do so.

I made my choice, and there's an end to it, she said to herself, watching through the kitchen window as Sammy strode contentedly across the field, swinging a milk can in one hand. I don't have any regrets. How can I? This is all nonsense, and I don't want to be reminded of it by seeing Gareth Llewellyn again. Ever.

Sammy had got her day nicely planned out. After helping with the chores around the farm, she and Joanna, Dai's and Bronwen's eldest daughter, who was her age, were going to take the ponies out for a ride.

'You don't mind, do you?' she asked her sister as an afterthought.

'You don't usually ask,' Carenza replied, with a smile. 'No, of course I don't. Have a lovely time. Actually, I thought I'd drive into Valley and post some cards. Then if it stays fine I'll go on the beach and read *Othello*.'

'Ugh!' Sammy shuddered. 'How can you? It's bad enough having to do all that stuff at school. Sorry!' she added with an apologetic grin.

'Lucky for me I don't have to actually teach *you*,' Carenza retorted. 'Such enthusiasm for the subject would be overwhelming.'

'You won't have to, since you take the A stream and I'm never likely to be in it,' Sammy said cheerfully—and truthfully enough, Carenza thought. Bright her young sister was—academic she certainly wasn't!

After breakfast, when Sammy had gone off contentedly with Trefor and Joanna, Carenza drove slowly along the winding, bumpy roads leading through tiny hamlets and past peaceful, lonely farmhouses, until she joined the road leading into Valley—or Dyffryn, to give it its proper Welsh name. Here she wrote and posted cards to friends at home, in the vain hope that they would reach them before her own return, and shopped for a few necessities—bread, a newspaper, chops and salad for the evening meal.

The sun was pleasantly warm now, and she fully intended going straight back to the beach to work on *Othello* and a suntan at the same time. She never knew what impulse caused her to pause and turn off along the road which led to the old Llewellyn house, Plas Gwyn.

Plas Gwyn was a stately Georgian mansion, its walls not actually white, as its name suggested, but a delicate shade of pale grey, surrounded by several acres of lush, pleasant parkland with oaks which had been saplings in the time of Elizabeth I, before the house was built.

Carenza parked her car, got out, and stood gazing at the house from a distance. All was quiet, and there was no sign of life. Old Rhys had kept a bad-tempered Alsatian cross who would lope down the drive, growling menacingly at anyone who got this close, but he was not in evidence today. Indeed, the place looked empty and deserted. Curiously, drawn by a magnetic force she did not recognise, Carenza advanced cautiously up the drive until she was within twenty yards of the front door. Nothing stirred. The windows stared blankly back at her, and, apart from the sporadic cawing of a brood of high-roosting rooks, there was no sound. She shivered in the warmth of the day. Living here alone in this great house was not a prospect she would have relished.

'What the hell do you think you're doing?'

She hadn't heard his soft footfall on the drive behind her, and, turning, was confronted, unprepared, by his hard, unwelcoming, suspicious grey stare. Gareth Llewellyn wore black cord trousers and a black sweater, and this garb, together with his accusatory manner and the harsh, disapproving line of his mouth, made him a stern, forbidding, deathlike figure.

Carenza jumped guiltily, well aware that she had been caught squarely on the wrong foot. Although she was not doing any harm, she was uninvited, and had known that her presence would not cause any rejoicing.

She thought quickly, reasoning that he would not necessarily know she had heard he was living here.

'I'm not doing anything, besides looking,' she said evenly. 'I understood that the owner of the

house had died some time ago, and I was just
interested to see it close up. There used to be a rather
intimidating dog which made that an unwise course
of action, previously.'

'The owner of the house was my uncle, and the
dog, as is often the case, survived him by only a
few weeks,' he replied curtly. 'As you see, the house
is not empty. *I* live here, and I'll thank you not to
call on me unless expressly invited to do so. Which,
I might add, is unlikely to happen.'

Carenza caught her breath at his brusqueness.
Well, she thought, one could not accuse him of
failing to speak plainly.

'I'm sorry about your uncle, and for intruding,'
she said, deciding the best defence was to shame
him by being courteous herself, even if he were not.

He did not seem overly impressed by these tactics.
Inclining his head slightly, he said, 'I hardly knew
him. The house was left to me by default—there
was no one else.' There was the briefest of wry
grimaces, then his face hardened again, becoming
haunted and bitter. 'As to your intrusion, I ask
nothing of anyone, other than to be left in peace.
Is it too much for you to respect that wish?'

Carenza drew herself up. An angry remark about
a little politeness costing nothing hovered on her
lips, but something forestalled her. To live here, in
seclusion, repelling callers and seeing no one, a fit,
active man in the prime of his years—as Gareth
Llewellyn clearly was—must be in some kind of
emotional trouble or distress. It simply wasn't
natural, otherwise.

She said slowly, 'You mean to say you live here,
all the time, completely alone? Without anyone?'

'Apart from the woman who comes in to clean,' he admitted. 'I avoid her, if I can. She talks too much—fortunately, mostly in Welsh, which, in spite of my ancestry, I don't understand too well.'

Carenza shook her head in disbelief. She thought of Dai's and Bronwen's farmhouse, loud with laughter and argument and banter, warm but sometimes overpowering. And of her flat, where you could hear the banging of other people's doors and the noise of other people's TV sets, Sammy and her friends playing their loud pop music. There were times when she had longed wistfully for a little solitude and privacy.

But not in such long, unrelieved stretches as this man seemed to desire, shunning all human contact, avoiding his fellow men—and women.

'That's ... that's incredible,' she murmured faintly.

'It's the way I like it,' he said bluntly. 'I'd thank you to remember that, in future.'

'Don't worry!' Carenza exclaimed feelingly, anger at last getting the better of her. 'I doubt I'll be back—even if expressly invited!' she could not resist adding slyly.

Something glimmered briefly in his eyes. It might have been long-suppressed humour, or grudging respect, but it was gone before Carenza could analyse it.

'Then we should both be well satisfied, shouldn't we?' he said, the beautiful voice dry with disdain. And as she continued to stand, staring at him in growing, incredulous fury, he said pointedly, 'Goodbye.'

Carenza did not give him the courtesy of a reply.
She did not think he had earned it. Turning
abruptly, she strode off down the drive, and did
not look back, even from the safety of her car, to
see if he was still watching to ensure her departure.

Awful, odious man! Let him rot alone in his
empty house, glaring at anyone who came too close,
if that was what he chose to do. He deserved to be
lonely, the way he behaved towards others!

But it didn't add up. This same man had once
acknowledged the applause of thousands, had given
unstintingly of himself, his energy and his sublime,
God-given talent. How could he turn his back on
a way of life which by its very nature demanded
communication and an outflowing generosity of the
human spirit?

Whatever could have happened to bring about
this catastrophic reversal? The puzzle nagged insistently at Carenza and would not let go, and no
amount of telling herself it was none of her concern,
and she didn't care anyhow, made an ounce of
difference.

Gareth Llewellyn haunted her all the way back
across the Menai Straits and through the moun-
tainous silence of Snowdonia, and, with her key in
her own door, her feet securely back on the firm,
unromantic ground of her everyday life, he still had
not released his mysterious hold.

# CHAPTER TWO

THE corridors of Longbridge Comprehensive had that same unmistakable smell of dust and chalk, Carenza decided with a smile as she sniffed the air, the indestructible aroma of 'school' which a mere half-term's closure had certainly done nothing to dispel.

She slipped into the staff-room for a well-earned break, to find John Perrin, otherwise known as Perry, head of English and, when wearing his other hat, director of the Spotlight Players, presiding over the coffee machine.

'Mondays are always grim,' he said comfortingly, noting her preoccupied expression. 'When they come after a half-term, particularly so. How is 2B? Are they playing you up again?'

Carenza had, as a matter of fact, been miles away, brooding over the mystery of Gareth Llewellyn and his reclusive lifestyle. She swiftly recovered herself and gave her attention to the problems of school.

'2B is ... well, 2B,' she said philosophically. 'I think I drew the short straw last September when I agreed to become their form mistress, but I'll survive, and so will they.'

'You volunteered,' he reminded her, pouring coffee.

'Is that what you call it?' She grinned. 'Maybe I did, but only because I was new, and too naïve to know what I was letting myself in for! Never mind—did you have a good break, you and Lynne?'

She thought his usually open face clouded a little. The last time she had seen Perry and his wife together she had sensed a distinctly chilly atmosphere, as though they had just had an almighty row, and were trying valiantly to conceal the fact.

'I can't answer for Lynne. I don't know whether it's problems at work, or problems with the kids, or what.' He frowned. 'She won't open up. If I ask her if anything is wrong, she says no, everything's fine, but I'm sure it isn't.' He shook his head, and forced a smile. 'Marriage can be a minefield, Carenza. There are times when I envy your life its simplicity.'

Carenza allowed herself a small smile. Bringing up one's teenage sister alone was hardly that simple, she thought. But there was a sense in which she agreed with him. The darker complexities of intimate relationships between men and women scared the wits out of her.

'Don't forget rehearsal tonight,' he said. 'I want us to have a proper read through, and start getting everyone thoroughly into their parts. I hope you've been doing some work on that.'

'I've been reading all week,' she said. 'Not that it has helped me very much. Something about Desdemona is eluding me. I don't know, Perry— perhaps you picked the wrong person for the part.'

'Rubbish!' he protested sharply. 'There simply wasn't any alternative. Carenza, you have more acting ability in your little finger than the rest of us put together, and that's the simple truth.'

She looked up at him, surprised. He had never spoken that plainly to her before, and, although she had always trusted his judgement, what he said was at variance with her own doubts—doubts reinforced by Gareth Llewellyn's reactions.

'I ran into someone on holiday who put my puny efforts into proper perspective,' she said wryly. 'Gareth Llewellyn. He's living alone in a huge old house his uncle left him, a few miles from the farmhouse where Sammy and I always stay.'

She saw his interest sharpen at once.

'Gareth Llewellyn? You mean *the* Gareth Llewellyn? An actor of his calibre puts all but the very best in the shade,' he said respectfully. 'So that's where he disappeared to, is it? I know he hasn't performed on stage for over two years, although he's still nominally director of the company he formed—the Shakespeare Trust.'

Carenza thought that perhaps that was why she had not instantly recognised him. Two years was a long time for an actor to be out of the limelight. She remembered, now, the ecstatic reviews charting his meteoric rise to eminence, praising his electrifying performances and his equally brilliant skills as a director.

Perry was looking at her enviously. 'What a stroke of luck for you to meet such a great actor,' he said. 'I don't suppose he happened to say if he was considering returning to the stage in the near future?'

Carenza laughed shortly. 'It wasn't quite like that. We didn't meet at a cocktail party, or over tea and buns on the vicarage lawn,' she said shortly. 'I had the temerity to wander on to his property, and he virtually threw me off. He's an arrogant, ill-tempered individual, from what I could discern, even if he is a genius! But no, I shouldn't think he would be coming back to the theatre. He lives alone, as I told you, and seems to want as little contact as possible with the human race.'

'But surely you must know the story behind that?' Perry asked. 'Don't you read the gossip pages in the papers, Carenza? I thought all women did. Lynne can always tell me who's marrying, divorcing or sleeping with whom, among the celebrities.'

During the last couple of years, Carenza's own life seemed to have been largely taken up by finding a permanent teaching job, looking for a suitable place to live which she could afford to buy, instead of rent, and getting hers and Sammy's lives on an even keel. Much of what had gone on in the world at large during that period had passed over her head, she realised guiltily.

'No, I don't know anything about it,' she confessed, and suddenly all her senses were alive and clamouring. Here, perhaps, was the answer to the puzzle which had disturbed her thoughts and dreams since her meeting with Gareth Llewellyn on the beach.

'He was married to the actress, Celia Harman,' Perry told her. 'Do you remember her? It was said to be one of those exceptional marriages between gifted people. She co-starred with him in many of his productions. Then she went to America to discuss a part in a film, taking with her their two small children—not much more than babies. Gareth didn't go with her, for some reason, and Celia and the children were killed in a plane crash on the return journey.'

Carenza sucked in her breath, and her skin went cold with horror.

'How dreadful!' she breathed, and, forgetting what she had said about Gareth, minutes earlier, 'The poor man! He must have been devastated! Obviously he hasn't got over it, and there's no wonder he dropped out.'

'The shock must have been considerable, but it happened over two years ago, Carenza,' Perry reminded her. 'What is there for an actor of his stature, if he doesn't act? Wouldn't the best cure be working, returning to the medium where he is supreme?'

The bells clanged loudly for the end of break, and Carenza gathered up her books.

'I must go, Perry. See you tonight,' she said hastily, heading off to her next class.

She had no desire to delve too deeply into the subject of the loss of a loved one. After so many years, she still found it too actively painful an area to disturb. Not death but desertion had been the cause of her own heartache, and, for all it had been so long ago, she still remembered only too clearly the time when her father had left her mother, when she was ten years old and Sammy just a baby.

Just like that. One day he had been there, and the next he was gone—forever. Or so it had seemed to her, although, as she grew up, she realised there must have been a little more to it than that. But her mother had been utterly broken by his defection, and years of pain, of emotional and financial struggle had followed.

My mother never truly got over it, Carenza thought soberly, not until the day she died. Was that what would happen to Gareth Llewellyn? Was his life ruined, too, or could he still pull himself out of the abyss? He, at least, had his work to go back to.

Leading a group of lively, rebellious fourth-formers through the complexities of Jane Austen's eighteenth-century social world demanded all Carenza's wits and attention for the next hour. No quarter was given to a teacher who was not fully in control of her subject and her class, and, although Carenza sometimes thought the latter was the slenderest illusion, worthy of a poker player's command of bluff, somehow she held the line, and even enjoyed crossing mental swords with 4A. They understood better than they knew how rigidly structured the dance of courtship still was, how much or how little of one's feelings could be betrayed—and the absolute necessity of a good go-between!

Perhaps society has changed only on the surface, Carenza thought, stimulated by the exchange of ideas which, to her, teaching was mostly about. The deeper patterns ran the same course they'd always done.

She had a staff meeting after school, and didn't arrive home until after five, hoping that Sammy would have managed to peel potatoes and lay the table.

Their flat was in a solid, modern, two-storeyed block in an unpretentious suburb. It had been the best Carenza could afford to take a mortgage on, and it wasn't the sort of home she would have chosen for herself and Sammy, had money been less limited. For a start, the rooms were definitely not designed for cat-swinging, and she would have preferred a garden. But it was clean and in a quiet neighbourhood, and there was a pleasant park across the road.

It was a start, she encouraged herself, as she parked her car in the communal car park. Perhaps, one day, if she became head of English...but Perry would have to retire or get a headship for that to happen, and neither was imminent.

Carenza ran up the stairs, and, as she glanced into the kitchen, noted thankfully that potatoes and carrots were already simmering on the hobs.

'Thanks, love,' she called out, hoisting the pre-prepared casserole out of the fridge and into the oven with a smile. Well, you couldn't have everything!

Sammy grinned back. 'I thought it was very good of me, considering I've got heaps of homework,' she said smugly. 'But I knew you'd want to be off to rehearsal tonight.'

Her head bent over her books again, and then, looking slyly up at Carenza from behind the untidy fall of her hair, she said, 'Oh, by the way, Nigel phoned. He says he'll pick you up at seven and you can both go in his car.'

'He needn't have bothered. I was planning to walk, anyhow—it's such a fine evening,' Carenza said, struggling to suppress her irritation. Going with Nigel almost certainly meant coming home with Nigel, too, and, given that he was playing Othello to her Desdemona, people would soon start seeing them as a couple, which was not what she wanted.

'I didn't know that, did I?' Sammy pointed out reasonably. 'Give him a break. What's wrong with him? He's not bad-looking, and he can't help being a solicitor. I suppose it's a good job.'

'It's an excellent job—did you ever know an out-of-work solicitor?' Carenza demanded, torn between exasperation and amusement. 'There's absolutely nothing wrong with him, Sammy, love; he's a perfectly nice man, but it's just that he's not—that I'm not interested.'

'You never have boyfriends,' Sammy observed. 'Why not? The other kids at school are always asking me if you do.'

Carenza eyed her warily. 'And you tell them my romantic life is non-existent, I suppose?' she queried lightly.

'Of course not!' her sister exploded scornfully. 'I'd lose face awfully! No, I tell them there are so many men who fancy you that you can't decide, so you keep them all dangling.'

Carenza wondered briefly which was worse, being considered a dried-up prune, heading for old-maid status, or the Scarlett O'Hara of Longbridge! Maybe this revelation accounted for some of the giggles behind the covers of *Pride and Prejudice* that afternoon!

The Spotlight Players were an assorted bunch of amateur thespians. Nigel specialised in property conveyancing; Briony, who played Emilia, was a director's secretary, and Francis, who had landed the meaty villain's role of Iago, worked as a surveyor for the local council. The rest of the company, right down to those who were content to shift scenery and make costumes, was equally varied. There was no star treatment accorded to or wanted by anyone, and Carenza happily made and handed round mugs of coffee before settling down to read the part of Desdemona.

Perry was moderately pleased with this first proper run through, and most of the cast basked complacently in his approval, confident they could eventually make the production work. Carenza found she was alone with her doubts and her nagging dissatisfaction.

'Pay no attention to her. All this soul-searching comes from fraternising with the great Gareth Llewellyn,' Perry laughed.

She wished he had not mentioned it. Naturally, everyone was agog to hear about this momentous meeting, and Carenza was obliged to retell the story for their benefit. Reluctantly, she had to admit to herself, and not simply because she didn't come out of it all that well.

She found herself remembering the racing white waves, the deserted beach, and Gareth's brooding expression, the rooks playing havoc in the trees around Plas Gwyn, and his black-clad figure. She did not want to share these disturbing but memorable experiences with everyone else.

Not only was it something that had happened to her in that other world she always escaped to whenever she went to Wales, that world of sea and sky and peace, but, although everyone seemed to know Gareth Llewellyn's story, only she had actually met him, and, in a manner she recognised as being a little childish, she wanted to keep it to herself.

For once—because she always enjoyed their rehearsal sessions and participated whole-heartedly in them—she was glad when it was time to go home. But even that was not straightforward, for Nigel was intent on being proprietorial.

'Let's go for a drink somewhere,' he suggested. 'It's still quite early, and such a lovely evening. We could drive out to this little pub in the country I discovered the other weekend. I'm sure you'd like it.'

Carenza shook her head. 'I'm sure I should, but I ought to get home. I've a stack of homework to mark,' she excused herself. 'And there's Sammy.'

He gave a sigh of deep exasperation. 'Carenza—your sister is fourteen, and not exactly a child any longer. She and that school seem to be all you live for. It's time you broadened your horizons. You're a young, very attractive woman, after all.'

The familiar apprehension began to rise in her, and she was glad they were driving along well-lit town streets, not quiet country lanes where they could pull up and be alone. For all that, she wished they would hurry up and get to the flat, so she could escape from him, and from the way that this conversation was leading.

'Perhaps I like my horizons just where they are, Nigel,' she hinted gently.

'But it's all wrong!' he protested, pulling into the car park. 'Surely, some day, you'll be thinking of marriage...a family of your own? After all, you'll be twenty-five soon.' He wrenched the handbrake on fiercely and switched off the engine.

Perspiration broke out on Carenza's palms. Be calm, she urged herself. Nothing really terrible can happen to you, here.

'You mean I'll be past it, soon?' she said jestingly, using humour as a barricade to hide behind. 'Nigel, I'm not in the market for a committed relationship. I've got my job, and Sammy. It's enough.'

'I don't believe it!'

He reached out to take her in his arms and kiss her, and she put out both hands to fend him off.

'Nigel—no, please. We might be Othello and Desdemona on stage, but not in real life,' she said firmly.

Kissing led to other things, to deeper intimacies which ultimately led a woman to fall in love and put herself at the mercy of a man. A man who one day might run off and leave her alone, desperate and bereft. She had seen it happen to her mother. It wasn't going to happen to her.

The best prevention was not to set one's foot on the path. Every time a man came that close, started looking at her with desire, wanting to kiss and touch, the same sick, unreasoning panic started to well up inside her.

Wishing him a quick goodnight, she slipped quickly out of the car and ran into the safety of her flat. But she knew, with a kind of resigned dread, that he was not going to give up that easily.

Two weeks later, Carenza came home from school on a Friday night after a particularly trying week, and decided on the spot that she could not possibly last another whole month, until the start of the long summer vacation, without a short breathing-space. Exams were looming, nerves were fraught, and although she believed she had made it clear to Nigel that there was nothing doing he still persisted in telephoning and calling round, and she couldn't face that, this weekend.

'Sling a few clothes in a bag, and let's go down to Anglesey,' she said recklessly. 'Monday's an occasional day, so there's no school, and we can make a long weekend of it.'

Sammy's eyes lit up. 'You're kidding? You're *serious*!' she exclaimed ecstatically, and sped off to pack while Carenza swiftly made sandwiches to eat on the way, and organised a box of basic supplies for the caravan. Within half an hour they were in the car ready to leave, grinning at each other like two children about to play truant.

The midsummer evening was still bright as they drove through Llangollen, but at least there wasn't a bottleneck of traffic in the town's narrow main street, as often happened earlier in the day. The majestic peaks of Snowdonia loomed proud in the lingering twilight as they left Betwys-y-coed behind and began to drop down towards the coast again, crossing the bridge over the narrow Menai Straits which separated Anglesey from the Welsh mainland.

There was still a glimmer of light in the sky as Carenza drove through the farmyard, with Sammy alighting to close the gate behind her, but lights had begun to prick out the darkening base of Holyhead mountain, and the sea was a calm skein of navy silk stretched across the bay.

Bronwen was out of the farmhouse in a flash.

'Goodness, and what a surprise!' she exclaimed.

'A sudden impulse,' Carenza laughed. 'Sorry I didn't phone to let you know.'

'No problem. We're always here,' Bronwen said, handing her the key to the caravan which lived on a hook in the farmhouse kitchen. 'Trefor will be across in a few minutes with milk and eggs. Is there anything else you need?'

Although Carenza protested that there wasn't, Trefor brought not only eggs and milk but bread, bacon and a batch of buns freshly baked the same morning. He and Sammy sat in the dinette area, drinking cocoa, eating their way through the buns, and talking as avidly as if it were months, not mere weeks, since her last visit.

Carenza sat in the corner of the seating which formed an 'L' shape around the lounge, and watched the night sky, the shipping activity in the busy port of Holyhead, reluctant to shut the curtains and separate herself from the world beyond them.

When Trefor finally took himself off, reminding Sammy to be up for milking, Carenza tumbled into bed, wearily content, and slept more deeply than she had for weeks.

The morning dawned bright and hot, with the kind of settled, almost Mediterranean weather so rarely experienced during the normal British summer. There were more people on the beach now, sunbathing, swimming, launching canoes on the calm, pleasant swell of the sea.

Wearing only shorts and a strappy camisole top, her hair blowing free, Carenza walked the length of the beach and up the headland, from where there

was no landfall closer than Ireland. She followed
the coastal path for some way, with no company
other than seabirds screaming overhead, finally
scrambling down over rocky cliffs to a tiny, deserted cove where, with a shock of recognition but
no real surprise, she came upon Gareth Llewellyn.

He, too, was in shorts, and a short-sleeved shirt
unbuttoned to the waist, revealing a brown, finely
muscled chest with a sprinkling of hair, still emphatically black. Although he wasn't exceptionally
tall, he had strong, well-shaped limbs and a spare,
co-ordinated frame, untroubled by flab anywhere.
The ripple of pectorals and thigh muscles stirred
an uneasy sensation in Carenza, as if it were the
first time she had consciously studied a man's body
and, astonishingly, found it pleasing to the eye.

She found herself waiting in some apprehension
for the too-familiar blast of his displeasure at being
disturbed, the dark frown, the steely glimmer in
the grey eyes, but to her amazement he merely regarded her with a level, unworried gaze, as if he,
too, had been expecting her to appear at any
moment.

'Well, now,' he said evenly, 'if it isn't Desdemona
herself.'

He spoke with a mild humour, but none of the
scathing sarcasm she recalled from their earlier
meetings, and had come to expect. She returned his
stare cautiously, not sure how far this surprising
amicability could be trusted.

'Carenza, actually,' she said, and when his dark
brows rose questioningly she repeated. 'My name
is Carenza Carlton.'

'Carenza.' Spoken by him with that slow, emphatic cadence, it sounded like music, and once again a wave of some quite novel emotion swelled beneath her heart. 'What an attractive and unusual name.'

Although it was not, strictly speaking, a compliment, more of an observation, she flushed with pleasurable confusion, feeling as silly as a schoolgirl flattered by the teacher.

'It's Cornish, I believe,' she said. 'I'm not Cornish, but my parents were living in St Ives when I was born. There's a flourishing artists' colony there, and my father was one of them.'

It all came out in a headlong rush, exactly as if she had been waiting all her life to tell someone this story. The real truth was that she had always hugged it painfully to herself, and could not to save her life have said why she was unfolding it now, and to him, of all people.

He continued to hold her gaze, his eyes calm and measuring. She had the strangest feeling that he knew all too well how important to her this was.

'You used the past tense. Is your father dead now, or simply no longer painting?'

'I haven't a clue,' Carenza said, long-suppressed anger thickly underlying her light, flippant tone. 'He left us—my mother, my sister and me. Ran off with one of his models to Italy or somewhere, and that was the last we heard of him. The classic cliché story, isn't it?'

'To you, obviously, it isn't, or you wouldn't still be nursing so much hurt for something which presumably happened long ago,' he said, quite gently. Then, appearing to realise intuitively that she needed a change of subject, he asked, 'You don't live here all the time, I assume?'

'No, I'm staying with the Pritchards. That is, I come down as often as I can manage to, and use a caravan parked on their land.'

'Ah.' He was silent for a few moments, and she saw his lips twitch slightly. He did have a sense of humour that was other than black, it seemed! 'In that case, I take it that it's unnecessary for me to introduce myself.'

His embryonic smile called forth a wider, answering one from her.

'No, I know who you are, Mr Gareth Llewellyn, although I didn't learn it from the Pritchards, to whom acting is no big deal. This is a small, quiet corner of the world, and you have too large a claim to fame to pass unnoticed.'

He winced. 'I suspect you're a teacher. You talk like one,' he accused, with a glimmer of mirth in his eyes.

'Well, yes, I am,' Carenza said, her laughter tinged with a mild indignation. Was she starting to sound like a typical schoolmarm spinster? Was that what he meant? 'How did you guess?'

'I thought you must be. It's the ingrained authority of addressing a classroom,' he said, and she breathed out with relief. That wasn't quite so bad! 'How is *Othello* coming along?'

The ready, conventional answer would have been 'All right, thank you' or words to that effect. But oddly, she found she could not be less than honest with him.

'Slowly,' she said, with a wry smile. 'At least, I think so, although everyone else seems to be fairly happy with the progress we've made, including our director, but . . .' She hesitated, and the problem crystallised in her mind as she spoke.

'I think it's me. I'm not . . . I can't get to grips with it. I'm not Desdemona. Perhaps I never will be.'

'Maybe you're expecting too much of yourself, too soon,' he said.

Carenza bit her lip. She'd told him too much, confided more than he really wanted to know. Why should he be interested in her trivial problems? He had lived through a major personal tragedy, and still wasn't anywhere near over it. His family had been wiped out of existence, at a stroke. It had robbed him of everything, including, so it seemed, a brilliant career. She had had fourteen years to adjust to the loss which had shadowed her own life, and it still hurt. Yet she had been blindly aud-acious . . . or insensitive . . . enough to trouble him with it. And now she had been on the verge of moaning about her part in an amateur production.

She shook her head. 'Maybe I am. Anyhow, it's not important,' she said briefly.

'But it *is*.' His voice was low, but compellingly urgent, and suddenly he seemed transformed before her eyes. He drew himself up, became taller, mass-ively commanding. His bearing was military, but yet he walked lightly on the balls of his feet, and she all but heard the rustle of silken African robes around his shoulders. He *was* the Moorish general, Othello.

' "Oh my fair warrior!" '

Carenza stretched out her hand towards him, and the sunny, deserted Welsh cove faded away. She was in medieval Cyprus, greeting her lord and husband. He gripped both her hands tightly in his.

'"Oh my soul's joy!

If after every tempest come such calms..."'

And then the words came naturally to her as he led her, line by line, step by step, through the scene. This wasn't acting. She was a young woman, deeply in love with an older, vastly more experienced man who had lived fully and dangerously, a man whom she had nothing to give but her untried self, and astoundingly it was enough—he loved her, too.

'I cannot speak enough of this content;
It stops me here; it is too much of joy
And this, and this, the greatest discords
be...'

Carenza had done this scene with Nigel, a few days earlier. After each 'and this' the stage directions had indicated that they kiss, and so they had. Carenza usually had no problems with kissing men on stage. It was not she herself, but the character, who did the kissing, who was tender, passionate, loving. It meant nothing.

But Gareth Llewellyn slid his hand under the heavy mass of her hair, at the nape of her neck, and drew her towards him with a world of tender authority in the gesture.

'"And this..."' She was youthful clay in his knowledgeable hands as he touched her lips very lightly with his. '"And this..."' his lips brushed her forehead like the caress of a silken scarf '"...the greatest discords be."'

And on those words the voice deepened, the playfulness went out of his eyes to be replaced by intense and unstoppable desire. Her lips parted, her own eyes widened, and her mouth flowered under his; brilliant pin-points of delight spreading out from a still, glowing centre, in a corona of sensation and need. Her slim arms clasped around his strong shoulders, her breasts beneath the thin T-shirt were crushed warm against his chest, and all she had ever needed was in the circle of his embrace.

Only when he let her go, and she was Carenza Carlton again, standing on a Welsh beach, did she start to shake.

'You shouldn't have done that!' she gasped. 'It was going a bit too far!'

He did not move, but his eyes took in her quivering shoulders, her unsteady manner, her frightened eyes, and he gave a shrug of impatient indifference.

'You've read the stage directions. What do you do in your production? Peck each other lightly on the cheek, as if you're just dropping him off at the station to catch the nine thirty-five, instead of greeting a lover returned from the wars? This is a man and a woman in the grip of a powerful physical love.'

He raised an expressive hand, and instinctively she took a step backwards. He let his hand fall to his side, and shook his head incredulously.

'Good grief, girl—you surely didn't think I was about to commit rape?' he said, his voice deep with scorn. 'You have no need to worry, I can assure you. Women don't interest me any more.'

He turned his back on her, bent down and, picking up a handful of pebbles, began to skim them idly, one by one, across the sea's glassy surface.

Carenza stood, arms wrapped protectively around herself, watching him for a minute or so. But he seemed not merely to have lost interest in her, but to have forgotten she was there at all. Withdrawn into himself, reliving past anguish, of which she, unwittingly, had only served to remind him, he had no need of her, no use for her, and asked only to be left alone with his own pain, and his solitary endurance of it.

Nothing she could have said would have made any difference, so after a further minute, she turned and resumed her walk along the coast.

It *was* acting, she told herself, that scene he had done with her, although of such a high order that it wasn't easily recognisable as such. It had felt...real, as he held her in his arms...real passion had scorched through her, leaving her helpless with desire, and she had responded, surely, as Desdemona to Othello's love?

Or had she? Confusion swept her, so that she no longer knew where truth began or ended. It surely could not be that Carenza Carlton had enjoyed being kissed, thoroughly and demandingly, by this moody, troubled, unpredictable man she hardly knew? Impossible, considering that she stiffened if safe, comfortable Nigel put an arm around her shoulder!

Carenza went back to the caravan and busied herself with preparing lunch. That afternoon, she and Sammy went swimming in a sea that was invigoratingly chilly, despite the warmth of the day, and in the evening they ate a vast dinner of roast spring lamb, fresh vegetables, followed by sherry trifle round Bronwen's huge scrubbed pine table, rounding off the evening with a hilarious session of Trivial Pursuit and Monopoly.

It was all so normal, friendly and untroubled that Carenza did her utmost to convince herself that this was the way life *was*. But it wasn't—or, at least, that was only a part of it. Life had its darker, more complex aspect, shot through with mystery and elemental passions she only half understood, and feared deeply.

Men and women loved, hurt and left each other, planes crashed into the icy Atlantic, killing hundreds, lives were wrecked, hopes mangled and twisted, promises were left unfulfilled. Love was too dangerous to embark upon, because betrayal, in one disguise or another, lurked treacherously around every corner.

'You were very quiet, tonight,' Sammy called as she washed her face in the caravan's minuscule shower-room before going to bed. 'You didn't even complain when you landed on Bond Street with a hotel and I stung you for one thousand four hundred pounds!'

'That's because I'm getting old and staid,' Carenza replied facetiously. 'I no longer have your capacity for easy indignation.'

But she did not feel old or staid, she confessed to herself as she stared into the mirror on her bedroom wall. Her soft, dark hair tumbled around the bare shoulders her flimsy summer nightdress revealed; her lips quivered with the remembered, bruising impact of Gareth Llewellyn's mouth. As she stood there, she lived a brief, dark fantasy in

which he came up behind her, laid both hands on
the naked skin of her shoulders, and pressed his
lips warmly to the back of her neck, just below the
collar-bone. As no man had ever done before. As
she had wanted no man to do. And then, lifting
her in those strong arms, turned towards the
bed——

'No!' Carenza exclaimed aloud. This was idiocy!
She must have been out in the sun too long, or
perhaps Bronwen had put too much sherry in the
trifle. The man wasn't interested in her, or in anyone
else—he was still mourning his wife. Nor was she
interested in him. It was all play-acting, a transient
madness of the imagination.

Carenza turned out the light, dozed fitfully
through the hours of darkness, but when she heard
the creak of Sammy's bed as her sister got up for
the milking she still could not truthfully have said
she had been to sleep.

# CHAPTER THREE

CARENZA had hoped that in the morning her mind would be clear and washed clean of all the disturbing nonsense that had troubled it. But after her restless night she had one firm thought in her head, repeating itself insistently over and over like a drum beat—I have to see him again.

To reassure herself that it *was* nonsense—that when she looked at him again in plain, ordinary daylight she would see only a man; intriguing, exceptional, touched with tragedy, but a man, not a figure of romantic fantasy.

To make it clear that she had not been afraid he was going to assault her, when she took that rapid step away from him on the beach. That notion was insulting to him, and made her look like a nervous ninny!

Two very good reasons, she told herself. But how did you make contact with a determined recluse like Gareth Llewellyn, who had made it clear on more than one occasion that your company was not desired, and who was not averse to expressing his need for solitude very forcefully?

Easy. You ignored all that, and called on him exactly as you would any other acquaintance. You got in your car and drove to where he lived, and knocked on the door. Which was exactly what she did.

But first, she prepared herself for the encounter by dressing very carefully. She had brought along only jeans and shorts for the casual weekend she had envisaged, but in the caravan's wardrobe she kept a few clothes suitable for various occasions, including a plain, crisp, shirtwaist dress in a creamy, linen-like fabric which served for any semi-formal emergencies which arose.

'Strewth!' Sammy said irreverently as Carenza emerged from her bedroom wearing the dress and the plain beige court shoes that completed the outfit. 'You usually only wear that to go to church! *And* you've put your hair up. Is the Queen coming to lunch?'

Carenza pulled a face at her. 'Don't be cheeky. I'm going to pay a call on someone, and, before you ask who, it's none of your business.'

'It's a feller!' her sister said hopefully, her eyes lighting up. 'Is he dishy?'

'Yes—no! That is, yes, it is a man, and yes, I suppose he's good-looking, but no, it isn't what you're thinking,' Carenza insisted firmly. 'It's just someone I know slightly, and have to go and see. I don't suppose you'll be around the caravan much today, anyhow, so you won't miss me.'

'No, I've got better things to do, as well,' Sammy assured her with a grin. 'If you're not back before dark, do I send for the police?'

'I'll be back well before then,' Carenza promised ominously. Slung out on my ear, most likely, she thought. Why am I doing this? Midsummer madness?

But she was cursed with a peculiar obstinacy, and when she had once decided on a course of action could not rest until she had seen it through. She drove out to Plas Gwyn, and instead of parking at the bottom of the drive she drove boldly up to the house and stopped outside the front door.

Her footsteps sounded loudly on the drive, and it seemed to Carenza that even the quarrelsome colony of rooks stopped cawing to watch this unprecedented event. Her own heart began to pound unreasonably as she raised the door knocker, and again she asked herself, why? None of her reasons sounded sensible or even honest now. She was here because of a compelling curiosity, and more—a need to see him again that she was unable to resist.

Her knock sounded imprudently loud in the silence all around her. Nothing happened, and she thought, relief struggling with disappointment, he isn't in. There was no sign of a car, except for her own, although, of course, there had to be a garage somewhere out of sight around the back.

Perhaps he was out somewhere on one of his solitary walks. Or perhaps—she cringed—he was inside the house after all, had observed her arrival and simply decided to ignore it and wait for her to go away.

Which was exactly what she would do, she decided thankfully. It was a crazy impulse which had brought her here in the first place.

About to turn, she suddenly heard footsteps approaching the door on the other side. A sick, nervous apprehension gripped her, her mind went completely blank, and she had no idea what she should say or do when he opened the door, as it was now obvious he was about to do. If she could have turned and run now, without looking utterly ridiculous, she would gladly have done so.

'Well?'

He wore burgundy pyjama trousers, in what looked like silk, and a Paisley print robe of the same material, knotted loosely enough around the waist to reveal that he was not wearing the pyjama top. His hair was tousled and his proud features were shadowed by a forbidding frown that would have deterred an invading army.

Carenza stood, five feet six, slim and lonely-looking, on his doorstep in her neat cream dress, her upswept hair revealing her long, straight neck, and pearl studs drawing attention to her small, beautifully shaped ears. She was trembling inwardly with nervousness and a swift-running excitement, because in all her quiet, circumscribed life, this was just about the craziest, most unpredictable thing she had ever done.

And since she could think of nothing else appropriate or sensible to remark, she said simply, 'Good morning.'

'Is it?' he asked doubtfully, gazing out at the cerulean sky, loud with birdsong, the trees lightly rustled by the merest breeze, the sun sparkling on the grass. A morning sent straight from heaven, if ever there was one, but he looked tired and drawn, a greyness beneath the tan of his face, his eyes blank and emotionless. 'You'll excuse the attire, but I didn't have the best of nights,' he drawled.

That makes two of us, Carenza thought, although she didn't fool herself that she was the reason for his lack of sleep.

'However,' he went on acidly, 'since I don't recall inviting you, you can hardly complain. Perhaps you *can* explain precisely why I find you on my doorstep?'

Carenza was briefly distracted, fascinated by his use of words, by the way he employed his speaking voice as a perfect instrument of expression. As soft as a caress, but with a whiplash of disapproval that stung hard, as it was fully intended to do.

She could mumble an apology and slink away, or she could brazen it out. Either way, she thought, he wasn't going to give her any help, so she decided she might as well be hung for a sheep as a lamb, and chose the latter.

'I decided to pay you a courtesy call,' she said brightly. 'People do it all the time, especially when someone new moves into the district.'

A sour smile touched the edges of his expressive mouth. 'People have never been encouraged to call at Plas Gwyn,' he observed. 'I am merely carrying on a tradition.'

For a moment she thought he was going to slam the door right in her face. Then he stepped aside and performed an elaborate bow, almost a stage obeisance.

'"Won't you come into my parlour?"' he invited, a world of warning in his voice.

'Said the spider to the fly', Carenza finished silently, not without a shiver of fear. She did not need telling that Gareth Llewellyn was not as other men. There were too many things which set him apart—his darkly brooding persona, his massive talent, the aura of tragedy which hung over his life. But she could not bring herself to retreat now, so she stepped past him, head up, shoulders erect, into the house.

The hall of Plas Gwyn was a rich, dark parquet which looked as if the woman who came in to clean kept it well polished. There was no furniture other than a small table on which stood an antique ebony and gilt telephone, with the receiver off the hook, she noted.

No one had seen her come here. No one knew where she was. She had walked in uninvited on this man, and, finding him still in his pyjamas, had not, as would perhaps have been proper, taken herself off. He could construe her choosing to stay in any number of ways, including the obvious one—that she was a theatrical groupie who was intent on throwing herself at him. She was aware that such things must happen to men as attractive and famous as he. In his present frame of mind, how would he react if he thought she was one of that species?

'There's no need to look so worried. I'm not un-balanced or anything,' he said softly, amusedly, and she thought guiltily that either her face was too re-vealing or he had an uncanny gift for mind-reading. 'Come through to the kitchen. There's probably coffee, if nothing else.'

She followed him down the hall, along another corridor and into a large, bright kitchen that sur-prised her with its gleaming, melamined modernity.

'Bit of a monstrosity, isn't it?' he said. 'Appar-ently my uncle couldn't keep his housekeepers, and he had the kitchen renovated to persuade the last one to stay.'

She found her voice at last. 'It doesn't really go with the house,' she agreed. 'It cries out for natural wood and copper pans—a country look. But I should imagine it's easy to keep clean and work in.'

He switched on the electric kettle and hunted for two cups and saucers. 'There are too many cupboards. I can't *find* anything,' he complained mildly. 'I suppose I don't spend too much time in here.'

He certainly had the air of a man set down in someone else's house, Carenza thought, watching him search out spoons and sugar, and a nagging suspicion crept up on her that he did not take very good care of himself.

'But surely you eat, so you must use the kitchen then?' she suggested.

'Eat?' He repeated the last word as if it described some weird, esoteric activity. 'Well, yes, I do, of course.'

But not with any great thought or regularity, she suspected.

'Have you had breakfast this morning, yet?'

'Breakfast?' He ran a lean hand through the tousled black locks. 'Lord, no, I can't be bothered with that,' he replied testily. 'All that trouble first thing in the morning—it's hardly worth it.'

'Nonsense,' she heard herself chiding him sternly. 'A good breakfast is an essential start to the day.'

Amazed at herself, but responding to an age-old female instinct to nurture, she opened the fridge, searched the cupboard for pans, switched on the grill.

'You've got plenty of food in here—bacon, eggs, tomatoes. This bread isn't too fresh, but I dare say it will toast,' she mused. 'Do you have a whisk? Yes, here it is.'

He perched on a stool at the breakfast bar, arms folded, and she avoided his indignantly watchful gaze as she whipped up scrambled eggs, grilled bacon and tomatoes, popped slices of bread in the toaster. It was all ready very quickly—she was expert at preparing this meal in a hurry before she and Sammy set off for school—and she slid the plate in front of him with a flourish.

'Damn you for an interfering female!' he said accusingly. 'Who says I wanted to eat, anyhow?'

But he did, she noticed, sliding tentatively on to the stool opposite him and sipping her coffee. It all disappeared very rapidly, down to the last slice of toast, and she wondered when was the last time he had eaten properly.

'For a man who doesn't eat breakfast, you haven't done so badly, Mr Llewellyn,' she remarked.

'Gareth.' He pushed his plate aside and looked at her long and consideringly, really seeing her, as if, until this moment, he could have passed her in the street without knowing her. 'Well, if you insist on calling me Mr Llewellyn, I can hardly call you Carenza. And it's such a pretty name.'

This unexpected pleasantry threw her into confusion, and she covered it by saying quickly, 'Would you like some more coffee?' before she had realised that he was the one who should by rights have asked that question.

'Yes, please, miss,' he said gravely.

Laughing at her secretly was probably an improvement on looking morose and gloom-wrapped, but it left her feeling foolish and uncertain. He disconcerted her more than anyone she had ever known.

'Let's get out of here,' he said with a distasteful shudder. Carenza had no choice but to follow him, coffee-cup in hand, back down the corridor and into a drawing-room that stunned her with its spacious proportions.

The furniture was solid Victorian stuff that Rhys Llewellyn must have inherited from his forebears, but the room was so large the heavy mahogany sideboards and brocaded sofas did not give an impression of overcrowded clutter. There still seemed to be acres of good Turkey carpet leading across to floor-to-ceiling windows, swathed in thick velvet drapes, and a delicate tracery of conservatory beyond.

The other side of the conservatory stretched to what was not as much a garden as a landscaped park after the fashion of Capability Brown, with trees and grass in a natural setting, studded with clumps of bluebells, leading down to a small lake.

'How delightful!' Carenza exclaimed spontaneously. 'It looks as if it just grew that way.'

'Most of the time, it does,' Gareth said ruefully. 'A man comes to cut the grass occasionally, but that's all. There's a more formal garden out of sight round the side of the house, but, frankly, it's a mess.'

Carenza looked up sharply at him. 'But don't you——?' she began, then checked herself. He caught on quickly, as she was beginning to learn.

'Find solace in the soil? No. I'm not really a countryman by inclination,' he said. 'Basically, I camp here. I use the kitchen—from time to time—

this room, and one of the bedrooms. Yes, I know it's a waste, but that's all I require, and the main point of living here is its isolation. Or so I thought.'

It wasn't hard to catch the meaning behind those words.

'I'm sorry,' she said. 'I shouldn't have come. I won't disturb your privacy again, I promise.'

He shrugged. 'At least you cook well,' he said. 'You paid your entrance fee.'

It was, she thought, a slight modification of his earlier hard stance, an indication that her intrusion had not been entirely unpleasant. But he did not extend her an invitation to come again, she noted with a stab of regret.

'I wanted to say that ... perhaps I over-reacted a bit, yesterday, when we were doing the scene from *Othello*,' she said quickly, striving to express her feelings without directly referring to that kiss. 'I realise that it was only acting, of course; nothing more.'

'Of course. Nothing more,' he echoed, with that way he had of paraphrasing words so that they became something different, as if he were forever seeking a new way a line could be said. He was silent for a long pause, and then he said, 'Desdemona hasn't eluded you. You had the essence of her in those few moments, yesterday.'

'You really mean that?' She frowned a little, flattered but unsure.

'I don't dish out silly compliments about things that really matter,' he said flatly. For a while he seemed to be formulating his thoughts, and she was wise enough not to interrupt, to sense that what he said would be important to her.

'The thing to realise about Desdemona is that she's the one character in the play who is exactly what she appears to be,' he said. 'She really *is* pure and sincere, her love *is* genuine, her heart *is* kind. Don't look for dark undercurrents—there are none. But the essence of her is courage. Think about it— for a young, sheltered, gently bred girl of her time to defy her father and society to marry a black general twice her age, that took guts!'

He looked down at her, and a smile chased fleetingly across the tired, world-weary face.

'There's also a certain sensuality,' he said. 'The love between these two is of the flesh as well as of the spirit. Let it blaze out, Carenza. Then when Othello thinks, wrongly, that she's sleeping with one of his officers, not a man or woman in the audience will misunderstand the sexual nature of his jealousy.'

He spoke calmly and succinctly but with such a deep knowledge of his subject, and a shining, unextinguished enthusiasm for it, that she lost all embarrassment.

'Thank you,' she said. 'You've made me look at the role—at the whole play—with different eyes. It will help, I'm sure of it.'

'You're welcome.' He took her empty cup and, setting it down on a mahogany whatnot, led her back across the room to the door. 'Work on it. Think about it—it will come. But don't,' he warned, as she followed him half-regretfully back down the corridor towards the front door, 'don't come back here for a fresh interpretation if you get stuck. I'm not your director. I'm through with all that.'

He opened the door, and the light streamed in from the breathtakingly sunny day outside, falling full on his dark, lined face in which the curiously light grey eyes were beacons of warning.

The admonition he had given her was too plain, too blunt to be misunderstood. Don't come back. He didn't want to be bothered any further with her characterisation of Desdemona, didn't want to be drawn, even on a casual basis, back towards the life he had forsaken.

'Oh, I'll stay away, if that's what you want,' she cried, mortified by his assumption that she might continue to pester him unless warned off. 'But although you probably don't want my opinion I have to tell you that I think what you're doing is insane. Ridiculous!'

A dangerous silence fell. And then, in a menacingly light voice, he said carefully, 'Oh? And what exactly *am* I doing, Carenza, that you, in your great wisdom, consider so foolish?'

Anger flushed her cheeks at his ever-so-patronising scorn.

'You know what I mean. Burying yourself here like a hermit. Avoiding people. Turning your back on the stage.'

His face was closed and dark, denying her permission to go on, but she could not hold back now. She was propelled by a passionate conviction of her own rightness.

'Gareth, you have a heaven-sent ability, a gift it isn't your right to deny the world,' she said earnestly. 'I know you've...' She faltered, but the subject could hardly be avoided '... I know you've suffered, but is this the way to deal with it?

Wouldn't it . . . wouldn't it be better to immerse yourself in work . . . to live again for the theatre and for the audiences who miss you?'

The tentative friendliness, the brief glimmerings of rapport that had begun to stir between them as he ate the food she had cooked for him, and as they looked out over the peaceful garden, all vanished in an instant. He looked at her as he might at a creature from another planet, who could not begin to understand the rules by which his own functioned.

'You, my sweet Carenza, are talking out of the top of your inexperienced head,' he told her coldly, lightly. 'You'll save yourself a lot of trouble if you avoid pronouncing judgement on matters of which you know little.'

If he had been furiously angry, if he had shouted at her or thrust her forcibly out, it would have been easier to take than this frozen assumption that all he had been through was so far beyond her comprehension that talking about it was a waste of time.

'I didn't mean——' she began hesitantly.

'Oh, doubtless you meant well,' he said icily. 'That's no defence. How dare you lecture me how best to cope with a grief you can't begin to understand? Who are you to tell me what I have or have not the right to do?'

She made one final attempt to justify her audacity. 'I only——'

'You thought you had an infallible panacea. You're not the first to think so,' he stated flatly. 'That's why I'm here. I thought I'd be safe from well-meaning do-gooders.'

He was very close to her now, his mere presence
defying her the right to move, holding her on the
spot, incapable of struggle.

'You never even knew Celia,' he said. 'She was
bright and beautiful, like quicksilver. And talented. She was my wife, my lover, the mother of
my two-year-old twins—yes, I had a family, and I
lost them, too. Just babies—they had scarcely lived,
and I shall never know how they would have looked
at five . . . at ten . . . at eighteen.'

Carenza's throat was tight with unbearable
emotion. She would not have spoken then to save
her life; the anguish emanating from him was so
strong there was no word of comfort which would
not have been a useless platitude.

'Celia was more than just my wife,' he went on
soberly. 'She was my partner on stage, too. I can't
replace her in either role. So you see, just as I know
I can't ever love another woman . . . so I know that
I can never act on stage again.'

His voice was calm and patient now, as if it were
a self-evident scientific process he was explaining.
But Carenza, who recognised the syndrome, saw
that he had retreated behind a barricade where he
hoped to be safe from hurt, from emotion. He was
all but unreachable.

All but? Was there a chink in the wall, a breach
in the dyke through which he still felt, from time
to time, the touch of the outside world? His passion
for Shakespearian drama burned as strong as ever,
she knew from the way he had spoken. And, if that
was the path by which he could find his way back
to life, perhaps, one day in the future he as yet did
not believe existed, there might also be a woman

who could teach him—not to forget, he could never do that, but to love again?

But it was not her place to try to tell him that, and to be honest, looking into his bleak, coldly angry face, she did not dare.

All she said, simply, was, 'Never is a long time, Gareth.'

He stepped back, holding the door open still wider.

'You've satisfied your curiosity and said your piece,' he told her. 'That should be enough for you. *Now get the hell out!*'

# CHAPTER FOUR

CARENZA did try very hard not to think about Gareth Llewellyn once she and Sammy were back at Longbridge, and it ought not to have been so difficult. After all, she was fully occupied. The last few weeks of the school year, busy with exams and end-of-term activities, should have kept her too busy to entertain thoughts which were anyhow unwelcome.

But he persisted in coming back to her at odd moments, unannounced. Sitting in a tensely quiet exam room, watching the rows of heads bent over their papers, all of a sudden she would hear his voice—that wondrous voice—exhorting her, "This is a man and a woman in the grip of a powerful physical love... Let it blaze out, Carenza," and her scalp would prickle, as if the hairs closest to it were curling and stretching, the nerves plucked by an invisible but palpable force.

It was worst at night, when she would wake in the dark, lonely hours, under siege from the memories she held at bay during the daylight. His mouth on hers. That swooning, out-rushing sensation, encompassing her completely, until nothing else existed. She had never felt that when any man kissed her, on or off stage. On stage it was something that happened to someone else, which she did not think about or feel personally. In real life it aroused in her only feelings shading from distaste to repugnance. She could not explain, excuse or understand her response to Gareth's kiss on either level.

In the end she had to force herself not to dwell on it by deliberately calling up less pleasant reminders of their last encounter. His sober, uncompromising assertion that for him all women had died with Celia. His firm warning to her not to bother him further with her own problems. And his final, harsh, utterly decisive, 'Get the hell out!'

He kissed me—once. What am I getting so worked up about? she asked herself disgustedly. Because for the first time she had found it an enjoyable experience? She was not in any danger of getting involved, falling in love, being hurt and betrayed the way her mother had been, because Gareth Llewellyn was way beyond her reach, had she wanted him. If he ever did emerge from the shell into which pain had caused him to retreat, if he ever found himself once again attracted to a woman he would not choose a nonentity like herself. It would be someone from his own world— someone gifted, beautiful, larger than life. In short, someone like Celia. The brightness of his own light would extinguish any lesser mortal.

But . . . it was strange . . . every time she rehearsed *Othello* with Nigel it cost her an enormous effort to relate to him in the role. She worked at it, she really tried, using every technique she could call up, but still she knew she never remotely approached the exquisite wonder she had touched briefly on a lonely Welsh beach with Gareth Llewellyn. He had lifted her, drawn out some ability that was buried deep within her, so that for a few amazing moments she had *been* Desdemona. But she could not repeat it, she thought with frantic despair.

'I don't know why, all at once, you're being so hard on yourself,' Perry said irritably after one particularly trying rehearsal.

Because I want *more* from myself, I know it's there, and I want to be capable of it, and can't, she thought gloomily.

'Perhaps we all need a break,' Francis put in kindly. 'I can tell you, Iago's really getting to me! Everyone in the architect's department swears I'm becoming devilish and devious.'

'Then why don't we have a little more devilishness from you on stage?' Perry demanded cruelly. 'In that last scene you might have been discussing the football results with Nigel, not trying to sow seeds of suspicion about his wife's honour!'

'I say!' Francis gazed after Perry's glum, retreating back with a crestfallen expression. 'I wasn't that bad, was I?'

Carenza touched his arm sympathetically. 'He's a bit uptight himself at the moment, for some reason. We'll have to make allowances for him,' she said comfortingly.

'It's something to do with Lynne. They're not exactly getting along too well at the moment,' Briony whispered. 'You know she works part time for the same company as I do? Well, rumour has it that there's something going on between her and her boss.'

'Surely not? Lynne and Perry? They've always been the ideal couple!' Nigel said, shocked.

Carenza turned away, sickened, and made a great thing out of collecting up the empty coffee-mugs.

The church hall where they rehearsed had to be left tidy.

There it went again, she told herself. Men and women, hurting each other, deceiving each other. But—Lynne? A calm, sensible, mid-thirtyish mother of two, with a lovely home and a devoted husband. How could she? And if it could happen to Lynne and Perry then no one was safe.

They all started out, starry-eyed, falling into each other's arms, making promises of undying passion, but it didn't last. She supposed that her parents had embarked on the sea of marriage in a similar fashion. So had Lynne and Perry. What went wrong? Was there some inbuilt mechanism which caused the spark to go out?

Just occasionally, perhaps, it worked ecstatically. But even then, when by some miracle the spark endured, fate intervened to prevent two people from knowing perfect happiness for too long. Look at Gareth and Celia——

Carenza choked on the thought. She clattered the mugs into the sink in the small kitchen, turned on the taps and tried *not* to think about Gareth. Gareth in love. Loving someone with his whole heart and soul...and body. Wanting her still, in the darkness of the night, and knowing it was no use; she was lost to him forever.

'Cheer up.'

It was Nigel, behind her. She turned and forced a smile.

'Francis is right. We all need a break,' she said practically. 'After a few weeks away we shall all come back refreshed and ready to give *Othello* our all. Lynne and Perry are going to Greece. I'm sure the holiday will do them both good. Briony's probably mistaken about Lynne and her boss, anyhow.'

But her words carried precious little conviction. Nigel picked up the tea-towel to dry the mugs, then hesitated, looking down at her.

'I wish I could take *you* away somewhere, Carenza. Somewhere romantic and exotic.'

She froze. 'Now don't be silly, Nigel,' she reprimanded him lightly. 'All this talk about Venice and Cyprus in the play must have gone to your head! I thought you were off to the Dordogne with your sister and her family. Sammy and I are going to Wales—that's exotic enough for me.'

He grimaced sulkily. 'I suppose you're staying at that farmhouse in the back of beyond, again. It'll probably rain for a fortnight!' he said, not without a mean satisfaction.

'It won't. We're having the best summer for years. And even if it does I don't care!' Carenza declared passionately. 'It's so peaceful and un-hurried there. And Sammy loves it.'

'And you wouldn't dream of going away on holiday without Sammy!' he said, almost accus-ingly. 'One day, you know, she's going to spread her wings and leave *you*.'

She smiled gently. 'I know. That's natural,' she said. 'I shan't try to cling on to her when the time comes.'

Looking up into his face, she saw that it was useless trying to explain to him that she did not feel constrained by her younger sister. She loved Sammy. Sammy was all she had. But, while they got along well together most of the time, she ac-

cepted the fact that one day Sammy would want a
life of her own. That was fine by her, although, of
course, it was bound to be painful, letting her go.

'But I wish——' Nigel began again.

Carenza handed him a mug.

'Are you going to dry these, or do I have to do
it myself?' she demanded lightly. Nigel was sweet,
in his own way, and not unattractive either, with
his light brown, neatly brushed hair and blue eyes,
but she felt nothing for him beyond a mild friendliness she might feel for anyone.

All the same, he had made her think.

'We don't have to go to Anglesey, you know,'
she remarked almost casually the next morning at
breakfast. 'Money is a little less tight now. We could
take the car and go camping in Brittany, or something like that. What do you say?'

Sammy's face drained white with horror. '*Not*
go to Anglesey?' she repeated, shocked, as if
Carenza had suggested she gave up breathing. 'Oh,
please—don't say that! I don't *want* to go anywhere else! Please!' she had begged, with more
feeling in her voice than Carenza had ever heard.
'It's going to be such fun, this summer. Dai's
building a hut round the back where we can play
table tennis, and there's a new foal, and Trefor
promised we'd go to the sports centre in Holyhead
and do archery and roller-skating, and——'

'All right!' Carenza held up her hands defensively. 'Point taken. It was just an idea. Lots of your
friends are going abroad for their holidays, and I
thought you might want to do the same.'

'I don't care what they do! They can all crozzle
on a beach in Spain, if that's what they want!'

Sammy declared emotionally. 'Anyhow, Wales *is* abroad, in a way, isn't it? They speak a different language. I can even speak a bit of it myself—Trefor's been teaching me,' she added proudly.

It wasn't until later the same evening that Sammy came to Carenza as she sat marking test papers and said, 'Tell me I'm a selfish little bitch, if you like.'

Carenza laughed, pretending to wince. 'Such language! However, since I've been 2B's form mistress for almost a year I can't pretend not to have heard worse! But why? What have you done?'

'I mean about the holiday,' Sammy said earnestly. 'All the singles go to Ibiza and Corfu, and places like that, don't they? You could always take me down to the farm—Dai and Bronwen won't mind—then you could go on a package. You might meet a nice hunk.'

Carenza closed up the pile of papers with an emphatic thump.

'Listen here, you numbskull! I do *not* want to go on a singles package!' she said, with a shudder of distaste. 'I'm perfectly happy to go to Wales with you—in fact, that's what I want. OK? And I'm not looking for a hunk,' she added as an afterthought.

'Because you've already got one, where we're going?' Sammy asked slyly, but grinning from ear to ear. 'I *know* you have—that's why you keep sloping off on your own!'

Carenza made as if to aim a ruler at her, but inside her a warm, dangerous emotion began to spread out from her heart, creating a glowing circle.

She would have gone away somewhere else, if Sammy had expressed a desire to do so, but it would not have been her choice. Of course she loved

Anglesey, the sea and the farmhouse, the little shingly bay, and Dai and Bronwen, but that was a peaceful, comforting love, not this pounding excitement that made her heart race and her breath uneven.

On Anglesey, there was always the breathless chance that she might bump into Gareth at any time. Not that she would dare go to Plas Gwyn again—he had made it clear she was not to do so, and she would have to respect his wishes. But he would be there, she knew it. And who knew but that one day, walking on the beach, she might come across him? Just the thought induced in her a queer faintness, a trembling of the limbs, a dryness of the throat.

What *was* the matter with her? Was this the kind of silly crush on someone essentially unattainable that schoolgirls traditionally went through—a phase which she, in the throes of her father's desertion and her mother's misery, had somehow missed? Perhaps she was a late developer, Carenza thought ruefully. Perhaps it would be better if they went to Brittany, after all.

But she knew that they wouldn't.

School broke up, to an unbelievable spell of high summer, blazing blue skies and a continuous heat wave. They crawled through Llangollen at a mile every twenty minutes or so, car windows wide open, but admitting only hot air and petrol fumes, not a hint of a fresh breeze. Carenza thought longingly of the cooler uplands of Snowdonia. But they were stuck once again in Betwys-y-coed, and hit another jam as they inched towards Menai Bridge.

Only as they finally touched Anglesey did the traffic ease, allowing Carenza to pick up speed along the A5.

'They'll be like sardines in Caenarfon and Bangor and Colwyn Bay,' Sammy said cheerfully. 'Why don't they all realise how lovely it is, over here?'

'I don't know, kiddo. But it's their loss and our gain,' Carenza smiled as they turned off at Valley and headed towards Llanfachraeth. Past the road to Plas Gwyn. Her smile deepened secretly. He was there. She would see him, hear his voice again, that marvellous voice that spoke to her in dreams. What if it did only tell her to get the hell out? It didn't matter.

But she didn't see him. She had been there for almost a week, during which the glorious weather persisted, day after day, and had not even caught a glimpse of him from afar, walking the coastal paths. It began to dawn on her that apart from her deliberate visits to Plas Gwyn her meetings with him had been the unlikeliest of chances, that she could be here for a month, two or three, without ever seeing him. A heavy disappointment settled in the pit of her stomach, and she took herself sternly to task. What had she expected, after all?

'It's market day in Llangefni tomorrow,' she said to Sammy on Wednesday night, after deciding firmly to forget about Gareth Llewellyn and get on with her holiday. 'Do you want to go?'

'Sure—why not? I like markets. Can Joanna come, too?' Her sister had reached the point where she went nowhere without a friend of the same age.

They set off before ten on the short drive to the small, busy market town in the centre of the island.

The two girls giggled companionably in the back while Carenza drove through gently undulating country, populated mostly by grazing sheep and cows, with an occasional grey stone village or roadside inn.

The market was popular and always attracted a lot of people, its stalls occupying a large area at the bottom of the main street, and spilling over on to the pavements. Sammy and Joanna took off on their own, leaving Carenza to browse around, picking her way past waving forests of T-shirts and printed dresses, mounds of cabbages and beans and tomatoes, until finally she came to the bric-à-brac stalls, where she lingered happily.

All around her she heard Welsh being spoken, its quick, lilting cadence, the tongue-twisting consonants that made it as unintelligible to the English ear as Finnish or Hungarian. Although Carenza did not understand it, it seemed to wrap itself around her, comfortably, like a familiar garment she kept at a friend's house.

'There's an awful load of old junk, isn't it?' a voice spoke softly in her ear, in perfect mimicry of a Welsh accent. 'Indeed to goodness, and I wouldn't be buying any of it, if I were you.'

Carenza turned slowly, taking time to compose herself. Gareth. *Gareth*. In white twill summer trousers that emphasised the darkness of his skin, and a silky shirt the colour of burnt caramel. Tanned even deeper by the long days of sunshine, and with a twinkle of something she had never seen before in his eyes. Light-hearted, almost, but with a new purposefulness, the haunted look reduced to a mere shadow.

She smiled, her own spirits lifted by this unexpected insouciance, as well as by the sheer joy of seeing him.

'I thought you didn't care for crowds. You seemed to be the cat that walked by himself.'

'Ah, but you can be very solitary in a crowd, especially if they're all talking a different language,' he observed with an engaging grin.

'Some of us can enjoy that kind of anonymity. But aren't you afraid that someone will recognise you?' she challenged.

He shook his head. 'Not a chance. I'm a forgotten man,' he said unworriedly. 'Besides, people recognise pop stars and soap opera personalities, not Shakespearian actors.'

She listened for a trace of bitterness in his voice, but although she strained very hard she didn't hear it. Undeniably, there was something different about him today. He hardly seemed the same man who had virtually slung her out of Plas Gwyn. Yet, knowing how quickly his mood could change, she was cautious.

'You weren't actually considering buying any of this rubbish, were you?' he laughed incredulously.

'Scoff if you like, but yes, I was,' she retorted defiantly. 'I have a special shelf in my flat, full of small items I pick up at these markets. I know they're nothing valuable, just mementoes.'

'Hm.' He regarded her with mild indulgence, and poked about among the jumble of knick-knacks on the stall. 'If you must have something, how about this?' he said, picking up a small blue and white glazed china elephant. 'He's about the least awful object there is.'

Carenza laughed. 'I think he's rather cute. I'll take him,' she said.

'My pleasure.' Gareth handed over the money to the stall-holder, and presented Carenza with the china elephant wrapped in tissue paper. 'For the lady who cooks a mean breakfast,' he added, in a tone of deep significance.

The stall-holder, a tall, bearded Sikh, winked knowingly, and two elderly ladies near by raised shocked eyebrows at one another. Carenza felt herself blushing fiercely. *She* knew Gareth was acting a part, but his small audience were convinced otherwise.

'You're impossible!' she whispered ferociously, moving away as quickly as she could, and slipping the china elephant into her handbag. 'They think . . . they think . . .'

'They think I've bought you a present for services rendered,' he supplied wickedly. 'Since it was all of two seventy-five they must also think I'm a mean old skinflint.'

Carenza, still pink-faced, gazed up at him, puzzled by this flippant innuendo.

'Gareth . . .' she said uncertainly.

'Come on,' he said. 'You've seen it all now. Winceyette nighties for farmers' wives and T-shirts with silly slogans printed on the front. Let's go and have a drink. All the serious trading goes on in the pubs, anyhow.'

He took her arm and led her up the street, not waiting for her agreement. The pressure of his fingers was light but warmly authoritative on her bare skin, and she wanted the short walk to last longer, so that she could continue savouring it. But

I don't *like* being touched, she told herself, deeply confused.

The pub was crowded with farmers in from the countryside, arguing loudly in Welsh.

'What did I tell you?' he demanded, as he fought a way through to the bar for them. 'The market stalls are for the visitors.'

There was no chance of a seat, but they found a relatively quiet corner where they could stand without being jostled. Carenza sipped her white wine and soda while Gareth had gin and tonic. The limited space meant that they had to stand fairly close to each other, and again that strange faintness assailed her as she became aware of little things about him—the way his hair waved back from his forehead, the slight pucker of his lips as he smiled lazily. The concentrated alertness of his eyes, intent on their subject...and, at the moment, their subject was herself. It was a keener scrutiny than she could stand, but, conversely, she had no desire to escape it.

'I wish I knew why you are regarding me with such deep suspicion,' he said humorously.

'I wish I knew why, all of a sudden, you're being so unexpectedly nice to me,' she riposted. 'Is it simply because we're on neutral territory? I seem to recall we parted on terms that were barely civil.'

She heard herself slipping into her school mistress's voice, the one she used to bring a recalcitrant class to heel, but could not seem to prevent herself from resorting to this defence. But he did not comment on it.

'Ah, yes.' A slight frown tugged the lines across his forehead tighter, until, once again, his smile relaxed them. 'You struck a chord, you see. One I did not particularly want striking, but now I'm grateful to you.'

Carenza's long, slanting brown eyes widened in astonishment.

'You are? Why? What did I do? It seemed to me I only succeeded in upsetting you, and I felt terribly guilty about that.'

'You upset me, all right, but you made me think—jerked me out of my inertia,' he said soberly. He raised his glass, and, with a brief return of his earlier flippancy, told her, 'You see before you the new, reformed Gareth Llewellyn, to whose renaissance you have contributed.'

The contrast, the juxtaposition of seriousness and half-facetious teasing, threw her. She was out of her depth with this complex, many-aspected man, who left her floundering in a mire of dimly understood emotions.

'I'm afraid I don't understand,' she said quietly.

'Of course you don't. I'm not making myself very clear, am I?'

He laid his free hand very lightly on her wrist, the fingers just touching the spot where her pulse beat, and she was instantly electrified. The current rocketed along her nerves, making her aware of her whole body in a way she had never been before. Her skin glowed with vibrant life, she seemed to feel her eyes brighten, her senses quicken, as if someone had switched on a lamp in a room that had been dark until that moment.

It was too much for her. She drew her hand away, leaning against the wall behind her, and leaving six clear inches of space between them. She saw that he had obviously noted her nervousness of physical contact; he passed no comment, but did not touch her again, and now, contrarily, she ached for him to do so.

'I've decided to go back to directing the Shakespeare Trust—in the autumn, most likely,' he said. 'I won't act again, but you're right—I can't hang around for the rest of my life, doing nothing.'

Carenza was so overjoyed by this decision that she forgot her own complicated apprehensions in the delight of the moment.

'Oh, Gareth—I'm so glad,' she said, in a voice low with pleasure. The fact that she herself might have played a small part in his return to the theatre—even if she had only been the catalyst— filled her with a wonderful sense of achievement and elation.

'I thought you would be,' he said, 'although why you should care at all, Carenza, is quite beyond me.'

She could feel her cheeks growing hot again, and fixed her gaze deliberately on a point beyond his shoulder.

'I care because...the theatre can ill afford to lose a talent like yours,' she said. 'Once, I had ambitions to go on the stage myself. It...it didn't work out, but it still means a great deal to me.'

Her eyes were drawn back, unwillingly but irresistibly to his, and she sensed him waiting for her to continue, knowing, insisting, that there had to be more. Without saying a thing, he forced the words from her, almost against her will.

'Also, I don't like to see anyone unhappy, and I thought that you were,' she finished rapidly, in a defiant rush.

He swirled the remaining liquid in his glass, looking down thoughtfully into it.

'Happy?' He pronounced the word slowly, trying it for size and discarding it. 'Well, now, that's something else. I'm not expecting to be happy. But I can be...occupied. Useful. Professionally fulfilled. That will have to suffice, I think.'

All her pleasure drained away, as swiftly as if someone had pulled a plug. It wasn't, he was making clear, a return to a full, human existence. Only a partial truce with an unkind fate.

'I'm sure your company will be more than pleased to have you back at the helm,' she said in a level, practical voice meant to inform him that, so far as she was concerned, that was what mattered—his personal suffering was his own affair. 'I must go now. I left my sister and her friend wandering around the market, and they'll wonder where I am. But thank you for the drink—and the elephant.'

'Don't dash off.' He didn't touch her, but simply used the power of his voice to restrain her flight, and it was enough. 'I've invited a few members of the company to Plas Gwyn on Saturday, for lunch. Perhaps you'd like to join us.'

'*Me?*' She gaped at him, too overcome by sheer astonishment to react sensibly. He was actually *inviting* her to Plas Gwyn—to have lunch with actors from the Shakespeare Trust? She was tempted to give her own arm a sharp nip to bring her out of this crazy dream and back to mundane reality.

'It's the least I can do. I've slung you out un-
ceremoniously a couple of times, and I'd like to
convince you that I'm more or less human,' he said,
with a faint smile. 'If you would like to come—
around one o'clock, all right?'

If she would *like*? Carenza did not recall bidding
him a bemused goodbye and walking back to the
car, where Sammy and Joanna were already waiting
for her.

She, Carenza Carlton, English teacher and amateur drama enthusiast, was invited to have lunch
with Gareth Llewellyn and his colleagues—genuine
luminaries of the theatre whose names were almost
legendary. She did not believe it. It could not be
happening to her.

His conscience must be troubling him a little, because he had previously been rude to her, she realised soberly. He was doing this to make amends,
giving her this experience almost as a gift, because
he knew she would treasure such an opportunity
more than anything money could buy. He had not
invited her because he desired her presence, or felt
the need to see her again. After this, he would consider her account paid in full.

But, even knowing how very little it meant to
him, Carenza drove home on a cloud. That, in
itself, should have warned her she was moving into
waters deeper than she could navigate.

Maybe it did. Maybe she heard the warning bells,
and deliberately, foolishly, chose to ignore them.

## CHAPTER FIVE

NOT until Friday night did Carenza pluck up courage to say anything to Sammy about her lunch date. It wasn't that she didn't want Sammy to know, rather the suspicion that her sister would read into it more meaning than actually existed. But she couldn't lie to her—their relationship had always been open and honest—and, as she had feared, her suspicions had been well founded.

'You're going to Plas Gwyn for lunch?' Sammy squeaked incredulously. 'But no one gets inside there, ever! And this...this guy, he's old Rhys's nephew?'

Carenza gave a small smile. 'This "guy" is called Gareth Llewellyn. He's an actor. I've met him a few times before, he knows I'm interested in the theatre and thought I'd enjoy meeting some other actors,' she said, keeping her explanation as low-key as possible. It was the simple truth after all, she told herself.

But Sammy, fortunately, was momentarily distracted by another notion. 'An *actor*? You mean, like Tom Cruise or Michael J. Fox?' Her voice was almost reverent.

'Not exactly.' Carenza's laugh was wry. 'A stage actor and director. Not films, I'm afraid.'

She had hoped her sister would lose all interest then, but Sammy was too quick and tenacious to have lost sight of her main point.

'He must like you a lot to invite you! Do you fancy him?' she demanded hopefully.

'It's not like that—I told you,' Carenza insisted. 'Come on, Sammy, only in a fairy-tale would someone as celebrated as Gareth Llewellyn fall for someone like me! Real life doesn't work that way.'

She was stricken by the lurking wistfulness in her own voice. Of course she wasn't wishing, even in her wildest imaginings, that real life, for once, would oblige. She remembered that overwhelming rush of sensation when Gareth touched her hand. She had thought such feelings were not for her— that early bitterness and mistrust had crippled her emotionally, so that she was unable to relate to any man. Well, maybe they had, but, to her amazement, she found she was still capable of a deeply instinctive physical response.

That was all there was to it, she insisted firmly as she went to bed. Gareth was formidably attractive, in a thoroughly unconventional way, and he had such a powerful presence that it was impossible *not* to respond to it. She would have to be very careful, tomorrow, not to give any hint of the feelings he aroused in her—she could well envisage his half-amused, half-apologetic reaction.

'You know that little schoolteacher I invited to lunch at Plas Gwyn?' she imagined him saying to his colleagues. 'Really, it's too droll, but I think she's got a bit of a thing about me. Poor girl—what can one do?'

Carenza shuddered and turned over restlessly. Perhaps she shouldn't go? She could always ring up and plead some excuse. Was the phone on the hook at Plas Gwyn nowadays?

Not go? Who are you kidding, she asked herself ruefully, when you're so excited you can't sleep—like a child on Christmas Eve?

She was awoken early by a loud knocking on the caravan door, and, struggling to sit up, she looked blearily at her watch on the bedside shelf. Eight o'clock? She hadn't heard Sammy go out for the milking—well, of course she hadn't; it had taken her so long to go to sleep that she'd been out for the count. But if Sammy were back already, she'd use her key, so who...?

Carenza thrust her arms into her cotton dressing-gown in a sudden panic. Trouble—an accident—farm machinery—Sammy! The string of thoughts leapt together as her mind made the connection, and she was out of the bedroom, wrenching open the caravan door, before she was aware that she had moved.

And it was Gareth.

She stood there in the flimsy nightdress which all but disclosed the long, smooth lines of her legs from the curve of her thighs to her bare brown feet, one strap slipping off her shoulder, stretching the thin fabric tight across her breast, her dark hair tumbling unkempt and tousled over her shoulders.

'Oh——'

She gasped and pulled the cotton robe around her, knotting it at her waist, but still she felt naked and exposed before him, unprotected and robbed of her natural defences.

'This is a dire emergency, or I would not have troubled you,' he said, the grey eyes regarding her unrevealingly, giving no hint of being pleased or aroused, or otherwise moved by what he had briefly seen of her. 'I figured that since it was a working farm someone would be up, so I banged on the door and the lady pointed me in this direction.'

Bronwen, Carenza thought wryly, would make a three-act drama out of this!

'You had better come in,' she said, and he followed her inside, closing the door behind him.

Carenza reached for the kettle and lit the gas, with fingers suddenly awkward. Why was it that the caravan, which had always seemed roomy for her and Sammy, now appeared to be full of Gareth? It wasn't that he was a large or bulky man; he sat in the window-seat of the lounge area, one leg folded elegantly over the other, one arm outstretched along the back of the seat, quite at ease.

It was purely and simply the life force that moved with him wherever he went, magnifying all his emotions so that his despair shook her to the roots, his pleasure elated her, and always, always, that electric crackle of expectation and apprehension combined, filled her with a racing, insecure excitement.

She set out the cups carefully, aware of him watching her and trying to appear unconcerned.

'Lunch is off?' she hazarded a guess. 'You could have phoned. Bronwen would have passed on the message.'

'Lunch is not off,' he groaned. 'It's the cook that's off!' Seeing her incomprehension, he went on, 'Mrs Williams, who "does" for me, and had agreed to cater, rang me a short while ago to say both her children were down with chicken-pox and sorry, she couldn't make it.'

He smiled winningly at her as she passed him his cup of tea—a smile that could dissolve granite, she thought, feeling her ribs liquify beneath its warmth, just as surely as his hard, merciless frown could darken the sky itself.

'Left to myself, I won't starve, but I'm not exactly a genius in the kitchen. Help!' he said simply.

She suppressed a gasp as it dawned on her what he was asking. 'You want *me* to...to do the cooking?' she asked nervously.

He set down his cup, and spread out his hands in an expressive gesture. 'Naturally, I know that I could book a table at the Valley Hotel and take everyone there. They'd have a good meal, but it wouldn't be the same,' he said. 'Of course, if I'm asking too much of you...'

The note of flat withdrawal in his voice stiffened her courage. He had come seeking her help, and, although his manner was studiedly casual, she couldn't help but realise that his opening up of Plas Gwyn to his friends and colleagues was a vital first step in his planned re-emergence into the world. Her refusal would not change that decision, but he would go forward remembering that she had been unequal to his request, and suddenly it was deeply important to Carenza that he should think well of her—if and when he thought of her at all. It was all she would have of him, perhaps, after today.

'I didn't say it was too much,' she said quickly. 'What exactly did you have in mind?'

He shrugged. 'I didn't. I was leaving all that to Mrs Williams,' he said.

She thought swiftly. 'How about a buffet-style lunch? It's going to be a lovely day—you could open up the conservatory and let your friends make use of the garden. It's going to be too hot to be stuck indoors round a table.'

'Then you'll do it?' He got to his feet in a sudden excess of energy and enthusiasm and gripped both her shoulders hard, his strong fingers digging into them, charging her with a pain that ran fiercely into pleasure as he dropped a kiss on the end of her nose. She wanted to cling to him, her head fell back and she knew a sharp, unbelievable longing to have him kiss her again, full on the mouth, as he had that day on the beach. To have those hard, pain-and-pleasure-giving hands running over her, touching places she had always shrunk from anyone's touching before. She half closed her eyes, forgetting all her firm resolutions about keeping her ridiculous desires and emotions securely under wraps. This was Gareth, here, holding her, touching her. What else mattered?

There was a loud clattering of pails and kicking off of wellies outside, and Carenza jumped away from him as if the feel of him had scorched her. She did not dare look into his eyes, and turned swiftly to meet the bright, questioning gaze of her sister instead.

'Didn't know you were entertaining so early,' Sammy said, setting the milk churn on the dining table.

'Sammy, this is Gareth Llewellyn—I told you about him last night, remember?' Carenza said, struggling for a voice that was reasonable and unexcited. No role had ever been harder! 'Gareth, this is my sister, Sammy.'

'Hello, Sammy.' He held out a hand and shook hers politely, unpatronisingly, as one adult to another. 'I've called on your sister in my hour of need, I'm afraid, as I've guests invited and no one to cook lunch.'

She looked him over thoughtfully, making no secret of the fact that she was deciding whether or not to accept him as her sister's friend. Carenza squirmed—trust Sammy, always so direct and open. Then she grinned, much to Carenza's relief.

'Carenza's a terrific cook. She'll sort you out,' she assured him breezily.

'I'm relieved to hear it.' His smile answered hers. 'Perhaps, now we've been introduced, you would like to come, too? If you've nothing else planned, of course,' he added.

Carenza froze. Sammy, who knew her so well, watching her trying to conceal her dangerous, ever-growing attraction to Gareth? Sammy, who said what she thought and didn't care who heard it? With a guilty relief, she heard her sister say, 'Well, thanks, that's nice of you, and wouldn't the kids at my school be impressed if I told them? But I've promised to go on a picnic with Trefor and Joanna. They'd be miffed if I backed out now.'

'I quite understand,' he said gravely. 'And I don't expect your friends would be too overwhelmed, anyhow. "Gareth who?"' he mimicked, humour slicing through his sobriety like a shaft of sunlight through clouds.

Sammy giggled. 'You're funny,' she said. 'Excuse me—I have to have a shower. Carenza won't let me eat breakfast ponging of cows!'

Alone, they eyed each other for a moment, she cautiously, he with a kind of triumph.

'She likes you,' Carenza said.

'Surprised?' he retorted promptly. 'Because you still have your doubts as to my sanity? Perhaps your kid sister is a shrewder judge than you are, Carenza.'

The deeply cutting edge to his voice caught her off balance. Why should it matter to him what she thought? The truth was, her feelings were far more complicated than simple like or dislike, but she could hardly tell him that.

'I didn't——' she began, but he raised a hand, silencing her in mid-flow.

'See you at Plas Gwyn,' he said. 'Don't bother about drinks—I'll see to all that. Old Uncle Rhys kept a fantastic cellar. If I'd been as far down the road to ruin as you believed, I'd have drunk my way through it, by now.'

She watched him go, frowning slightly. The atmosphere had changed subtly after Sammy's arrival. Why? Moments before, she had half expected him to kiss her. Was that it? Was he saying, all right, I've set my foot on the path to recovery, but don't push me too far, don't ask too much? His whole attitude had her deeply perplexed.

Some time later, she arrived at Plas Gwyn, nervous but determined, after a trip to Holyhead, with a car boot full of supplies. Figuring she wouldn't have time to return home later to change, she had borrowed a flowery overall from an intensely curious Bronwen to cover the skimpily elegant red and white printed sundress she would be wearing to lunch.

'Cooking for him, is it?' Bronwen had said knowingly. 'No woman cooks for a man unless there's an interest. Way to the heart through the stomach, and all that.'

'He asked me. I'm merely helping out,' she had replied, stone-walling deliberately.

Bronwen had shrugged. 'No man asks a woman unless there's an interest on his side.'

'He probably doesn't know anyone else to ask, if he's been living as cut off from society as you say,' Carenza had said, fighting down an embarrassed irritation.

'He's awfully handsome, in a devilish kind of way,' Sammy had interposed. 'Very sexy.'

Carenza had been glad to escape. But here at Plas Gwyn was Gareth, still wearing a look of brooding displeasure with her, for some reason she could not fathom. And, as her sister had unerringly put her finger on the right word, sexy. Exuding a volcanic Celtic miasma of smouldering sensuality that was part of his persona, whether he chose to exert it or not, whether he was even aware of it or not. The tightly banked fires that on stage were sublimated and channelled, directed into a performance that forged you to your seat. And with a woman in his arms? It did not bear thinking about. Where did it go now, that force he had denied existence since Celia died?

She pretended to be unaware of his watching eyes as she put beef and chicken in the oven to roast, chopped salad, prepared marinated herring, smoked trout and mushrooms à la greque.

'Is there anything you would like me to do, apart from keeping out of the way?' he asked drily,

pointedly drawing attention to her brisk, supposedly preoccupied silence.

She looked up. His eyes were deeply searching,
and it was all she could do not to drop her gaze in
evasion.

'The big drawing-room—I'll need a long table
covered with a cloth, preferably white. Glasses,
plates, cutlery. Some chairs out in the conservatory. Flowers—if you can find some, I'll arrange
them later. Will your guests want background
music?'

'No. They prefer the sound of their own voices.
They're actors,' he reminded her with the slightest
of smiles.

It was a rush, but by twelve-thirty everything was
ready. The beef was sliced thinly and lightly dressed
in warm vinaigrette, the chicken was folded in a
cold, mild curry-flavoured mayonnaise. There was
a gâteau and cheesecake—'Bought, I'm afraid, but
there wasn't time to make my own,' Carenza said
apologetically.

Gareth had found several bottles of good Saint-
Emilion in his uncle's cellar, also a dry Muscadet
for those who preferred white wine. Other drinks
were arranged on a deep silver gallery tray, surrounded by Waterford crystal goblets. Fine Irish
linen cloths covered the table, and from the garden
he had brought in armfuls of roses and carnations.
'Running riot. I've had the gardener tidy up a bit,'
he said, bringing out beautiful cut-glass vases from
the vast sideboard. 'I'd no idea Uncle Rhys had so
much stuff. Even those little white wrought-iron
tables and chairs in the conservatory. I found them
in the garden shed.'

They stood back and surveyed their handiwork, the tension between them briefly dissolved.

'You have mayonnaise on your forehead,' he said gently, picking up a paper napkin. 'Here—keep still.'

Carenza backed away, trembling. She wanted him to touch her, and was terrified that he might, and that she might like it altogether too much. Might want more.

'I have to have a wash, anyhow,' she said hurriedly. 'Where's the bathroom?'

Racing upstairs, grabbing her handbag. Splashing cold water on her face, and then, with hands that fought to be steady, applying make-up. She'd come here to meet his colleagues from the theatrical world, a chance life would never offer her again. But all she could think of was Gareth, his eyes looking deep into hers, his hands on her shoulders, while the world slowed down and stopped. She brushed her hair out, fiercely. She had meant to put it up, but there was no time; besides, she'd probably make a mess of it, in this state. At least half of her wanted to run away—now, this minute.

She looked at herself in the mirror, and said out loud, 'I'm in love with him.' But she *could not* be. She had no idea what it meant, to be in love. And it wasn't supposed to happen to her. She was immune. Nevertheless, 'I'm in love with him.' She repeated it silently to herself as she went downstairs, and knew that it was already too late for denials or protestations. Somehow, she had fallen victim to the disease she most feared.

\*   \*   \*

The four members of the Shakespeare Trust whom
Gareth had invited—two men and two women—
arrived shortly before one o'clock, in a venerable
but still gleaming Mercedes driven by one of the
women, Beth Gibson, a formidable character actress in her fifties whom Carenza had seen many
times in high-class television drama.

'Good lord, Gareth, you certainly have seques-
tered yourself out in the sticks here,' she exclaimed, stretching her tall, angular frame as she
got out of the car. 'But the air is wonderful—so
fresh that you can taste it.'

Carenza found it hard not to stare at her lean,
mobile, expressive face with its long, firm nose and
wide mouth. Beth Gibson had never been pretty,
but she was possibly more striking now than she
had been in her younger days.

The man who had occupied the front passenger
seat was Melvin Parminter, slight, witty, agile; his
Mercutio in *Romeo and Juliet* some years earlier
had caused a buzz to whirr through the theatrical
world. Carenza liked his quick, ready smile and his
lively manner. The other man was tall and languid,
with a sombre, almost lugubrious face, and eyes
that twinkled wickedly in complete contrast. She
had only seen that face on posters, but he was instantly recognisable as Cyril Templeton.

That left one more person, a young woman of
about Carenza's own age, tiny, but with a vivid,
unmistakable presence, an arresting face, wide at
the forehead and tapering to a delicate, pointed
chin, framed by a mass of unruly blonde curls, *'au
naturel'*. Her name, and her face, had been everywhere this year, and Carenza reflected that it was

impossible to live on the same planet and not know who she was. Marianne St John—a rising star, ready to explode into brilliance at any moment.

Carenza stood tongue-tied with shyness before these luminaries of the profession, and it was Gareth who took her arm gently and drew her forward.

'Folks, I want you to meet a new friend of mine— Carenza Carlton,' he said. 'You'll all have good cause to be grateful to her, since she's responsible for the food.'

He introduced the others to Carenza one by one—the two men shook her hand warmly, and the great Beth Gibson actually kissed her on the cheek, like a favourite aunt. Marianne's handshake was cool and brief.

'Are you in the business, Miss Carlton... Carenza...? I don't seem to recall the name,' she murmured. It wasn't really a disparagement, but somehow she succeeded in putting Carenza in her place, setting her outside their charmed professional circle.

'No, I'm not,' Carenza replied shortly, aware that she sounded ungracious, but not wanting to parade her amateur status before these respected personages. It was better they thought she had nothing at all to do with the stage. 'Actually, I teach English Lit,' she added, in an attempt to be more forthcoming.

'Well, someone has to.' Marianne laughed in her silvery voice.

Mel took Carenza's arm as they trooped indoors after Gareth.

'Take no notice of her, darling,' he said lightly. 'She's been in a bitchy mood all the way from Birmingham. I think she must have been crossed in love.'

Carenza could not imagine any man rejecting the beautiful Marianne, so she merely smiled, grateful for his friendliness.

There were exclamations of pleasure as the party entered the drawing-room, where the long windows were thrown open to the conservatory and garden. The room had been brought to life by the warm, sunny air, the great vases of flowers, and the tempting display of food spread out on the long table. It was once again, briefly, a country house where someone lived and entertained, where guests were invited to stay. All it needed now, Carenza thought, with a sudden lump in her throat, were children running on the grass outside.

Gareth's twins should have been playing there. Glancing across at him, she caught the sudden shadow flitting across his face, and somehow knew the same thought had occurred to him. Then he put on a bright, convivial expression, and began to play the host, opening bottles, fixing drinks. Glasses clinked and there was laughter as Mel jumped on a chair and called for silence.

'Shut up, you noisy lot! This is worse than a chorus dressing-room!' he cried. 'I just want to say one thing—yes,' he protested, shouting down exaggerated groans from his colleagues. 'Welcome back, Gareth. We've missed you—and we need you.'

'Hear! Hear!' Beth confirmed with great feeling, throwing her arms round Gareth and holding him in a brief embrace. No sooner had she released him than Marianne did the same, but her embrace was subtly different. She let her small hands slide almost erotically up his chest, and, leaning her head back slightly, smiled up into his eyes. He didn't attempt to prolong this welcome, but neither did he withdraw from it, Carenza noted with a pang.

'See what a lot of children they are, really,' he said to Carenza, when he was free again. 'There's a child lurking somewhere in all actors—why else would one earn a living pretending to be someone else?'

'I can't imagine why we're all so overjoyed by the notion of having *him* back again, hectoring us, dictating to us—insulting us,' Cyril said, mock-morosely. 'I'll tell you, Carenza, he is a thorough-going tyrant. Napoleon has nothing on him, nor Ivan the Terrible!'

'Whinging already?' Gareth said cheerfully. 'Let's dispose of all this splendid food, shall we? What about some wine? Who wants white...? Marianne, I know you do. Red for you, Mel?'

He seemed in marvellous form, helping everyone to food and wine, talking and laughing with perfect ease. But, while Carenza did not doubt he was genuinely glad to see his guests, she wondered just how much of his sociable jocularity was a performance. No one could go from cut-off, silent recluse to sparkling host in one easy leap, but since he was Gareth, she thought, there were no half-measures. If he couldn't do it naturally, he'd act. And this small gathering, who probably knew all too well what he was about, applauded his courage inwardly, and joined in.

'Phenomenal, isn't he?' Beth said quietly to Carenza as they helped themselves to cold curried chicken. 'But don't be fooled. Celia's death hit him hard, and he's had to trudge a lonely road back from the wilderness. Have you known him long?'

'A couple of months, but only on and off,' Carenza said. 'I come down here for holidays, and we keep—er—bumping into one another. Well, to be honest, I invaded his solitude a little. I didn't think such loneliness could be right for anyone.'

Beth cast her a look almost of admiration. 'You're lucky you didn't get hurled out, bodily,' she said. 'People who've known him far longer have got short shrift over the last year or two. You must be very brave.'

'Perhaps my courage was only ignorance,' Carenza laughed, flustered. 'Still—it's good he's going back to you, if only to direct.'

Beth grimaced. 'Mel spoke the truth when he said we needed Gareth. We've hung on, kept it going, but we're all but falling apart. Gareth was... is...our helmsman. Our driving force. He has such energy, such passion. They say no one's indispensable, but it's not true. Gareth is a one-off.'

Impulsively, Carenza said, 'Tell me about her— Celia. What was she really like?'

Beth paused, and a guarded look came into her eyes. 'How to describe her? She wasn't pretty, in the accepted sense of the word, but she was so vivacious she made you believe she was beautiful. Incandescent. When she was in a room she lit it up.'

'They must have been a tremendous couple,' Carenza observed wistfully. 'Both on and off stage.'

'Yes,' Beth said shortly, and then, after a brief hesitation, went on, 'They certainly struck sparks off one another. When they did *Antony and Cleopatra* together, there was a full minute of silence after the curtain fell. I've never heard anything like it—it was twice as meaningful as applause. The entire house was awestruck. A moment of theatrical history.'

'I wish I'd seen that.' Carenza looked pensively across the room at Gareth, who was deep in conversation with Marianne. 'Now, perhaps, no one will ever know the magic of seeing him act, again.'

'I wouldn't be too sure of that,' Beth smiled slowly. 'There are those with a vested interest in persuading him, if you see what I mean.'

She said no more. She did not have to. Carenza could see it all for herself. The blonde actress had her hand resting lightly on Gareth's arm, her face at once innocent and voluptuous, tilted upwards to look into his eyes. Here was the successor, all ready and programmed to step into Celia's shoes, not only on stage, but into Gareth's empty heart. Marianne was waiting in the wings, and, if the shadow of Celia stood beside her—well, she was alive, and Celia was dead.

It wasn't fair. For the first time in her life, today, Carenza had discovered painfully that she could fall in love, like any other girl, and it had to be with someone as far beyond her reach as the nearest star. Someone who had told her plainly that he wasn't over the loss of the woman he had loved.

But one day, perhaps, he would be ready to love again, and here was the perfect candidate. If anyone could capture Gareth's love, then Marianne St John

was the woman most likely to do it, Carenza realised, a band of hopelessness tightening around
her heart. She was young, lovely, and exceptionally
talented, by all accounts. And when Gareth returned to directing the Shakespeare Trust they
would be working closely together. Touring
together. How could he not, one day, burn to play
Troilus to her Cressida? How could he not want to
take her in his arms and recapture the happiness he
had lost?

Then perhaps, one day, it would be Marianne's
children running out there on the sunlit grass.

Carenza turned away from the sight of them
together, a forced smile on her lips. You surely never
thought it would be *yours*, she told herself
scathingly. One kiss, a few desultory chats, and a
lunch party do not a meaningful relationship make!
He isn't yours. He can never be yours. So get a grip
on yourself, if you don't want to suffer needlessly.

## CHAPTER SIX

AFTER they had finished lunch, they all wandered out into the garden. The afternoon was hot, and before long they were all lounging on the grass, shoes kicked off. Gareth went round again with the wine bottle, and there was a lot of laughter, and, after a while, a certain amount of theatrical reminiscence, 'Do you remember that time in Bradford when . . .?' which led to discussions of productions and personalities, equally divided between bitchiness and generosity.

Carenza remained quiet through all this, content to listen with intent fascination, although she could not contribute, but Gareth, realising that she was a little out of it, said, 'Enough of all this shop-talk. It might be interesting to us, but it can't mean a lot to Carenza.'

'It's all right,' she said quickly, aware of an irrational resentment of his sympathy, because that was not what she wanted from him.

'Darling—we're actors. There's not much else we like to talk about,' Marianne drawled lazily. 'We're such a selfish, introverted set of individuals. I'm sure Carenza will forgive us if we bore her.'

'Carenza isn't bored by acting. She belongs to a dramatic society, and is about to play no less a role than Desdemona,' Gareth said.

She sat stiffly, wishing he had not divulged this information, sure that they could not possibly be interested. Marianne uttered a little half-derisory laugh, but the others at once began to bombard her with shrewd, intelligent and genuinely concerned questions about the society, the production, and her own part in it. Carenza was soon caught up in an avid conversation, and would have thoroughly enjoyed the interchange of ideas, had it not been for the presence of Marianne, who contributed nothing, but lay back with her eyes closed and a little smile on her lips indicating that all this was beneath her.

They talked theatre generally, asking Carenza what other roles she had done.

'I loved *The Importance of Being Earnest*,' Beth laughed. 'I was Lady Bracknell—what else? *"A handbag!"*' she boomed threateningly, and Mel and Cyril joined in her laughter. 'Gareth, we really must do some more comedy, soon.'

Marianne sat up, clearly bored with this. 'Gareth, what are you going to do with this house when you come back to work?' she asked. 'You obviously can't live here when we're based in Birmingham. Shall you put it on the market?'

Carenza could not prevent the sharp turn of her head. Sell Plas Gwyn—break the long Llewellyn tradition which stretched back almost two hundred years? Surely he wouldn't? The thought that Gareth might not be here, ever again, was deeply painful. Just to know that he came here sometimes, even if she never saw him, was reassurance of a kind—and it was all she could hope for.

'It's near enough for weekends,' she heard herself say.

'The theatre isn't like that, darling,' Marianne said patronisingly. 'One is either constantly rehearsing, or on tour. It's not nine to three-thirty, like teaching.'

It was on the tip of Carenza's tongue to retort that teaching wasn't always like that, either, but Cyril, who had been only half listening to the exchange, said suddenly, 'Celia would have loved playing the country lady down here, Gareth, wouldn't she?'

Her name had been spoken, and, although the sky was as blue and cloudless as ever, the sun as hot, a shadow seemed to fall across them.

'That's nonsense, Cyril. Celia loved bright lights and people—she'd have been bored out of her mind,' Marianne said quickly, the implication being that so would she, and Gareth, once he came back to his senses, would waste no time in putting Plas Gwyn behind him.

Gareth got to his feet abruptly. 'Celia,' he said with cutting incisiveness, 'could play any damn role she wanted, most of the time.'

Hands dug deep into his pockets, he strode off in the direction of the lake. Marianne made as if to follow him, but Beth restrained her, and it was she who went after him.

They stood down by the lake for quite some time, too far away to be overheard. After a while, Cyril and Mel took a stroll around the park, leaving Carenza somewhat uncomfortably with Marianne.

The young actress shook her blonde curls in a gesture of angry frustration.

'It's all rather silly, when you think about it,' she said. 'It's such a sham—all this business about Celia and Gareth that the Press cooked up, about their wonderful acting partnership and their equally wonderful marriage.'

Carenza turned her head slowly to look at the other girl. 'I'm not with you.'

'Naturally. You weren't around at the time. Oh, well, I may as well tell you,' Marianne said casually, as if it was of no great importance what Carenza knew or did not know. 'Celia was involved with someone else—an American film producer. That's why she went to Hollywood. We all knew about it, all of us in the Shakespeare Trust, who were closest to Gareth. Certainly, everyone who's here today knew.'

'And he didn't? How awful.'

'Oh, don't be naïve, *of course* Gareth knew,' Marianne said scornfully. 'He never said anything to us, but he's far too intelligent and perceptive not to have known.'

'I find it hard to believe,' Carenza said stubbornly. She did not know why it mattered so much to preserve her belief in Gareth's and Celia's unsullied love, but still, without knowing, she found herself defending it against Marianne's insinuations. 'Why... he still loves her, still mourns her. He couldn't talk... couldn't feel the way he does about a woman he knew was unfaithful to him.'

'He's kidding himself,' Marianne said curtly. 'Now she's gone, he wants to preserve the memory of their supposedly ideal marriage, and we all go along with the pretence! Didn't you hear what he said? Celia could play any damn role she chose. For him, she was playing the devoted wife and mother. Then she went to America and found a role she couldn't play.'

'I don't understand,' Carenza said cautiously.

Marianne gave a deliberately patient sigh. 'You really don't know much about this business, do you?' she said. 'Well, why should you? It's like this—not every stage actor can make the transition to films. In spite of being the producer's girlfriend, Celia flunked her screen test. She was no good without Gareth, you see. It was he who made her what she was, coaxed her performances from her. Her success was tied to his coat-tails. I could act her into the ground, any day,' she added disparagingly.

Since Celia was dead, there was no way of proving or disproving this statement, Carenza thought. She was still reeling from the discovery that the tragic story of Gareth and Celia had bitter undertones. No wonder he had taken it all so badly, shutting himself off from the world. No wonder he was reluctant to involve himself with another woman. What a terrible strain he must have been under, striving to keep alive for the rest of the world—and for himself—the myth of his partnership with Celia, on stage and off... while deep down, barely admitted, the poison of the truth ate away at him.

She said, 'He must have suffered dreadfully.'

Marianne gave her a queer look, charged with warning. 'Yes, but it's almost over. He's coming back,' she said decidedly. 'I know he said he won't act again, but he must. He must. He only needs a new lead.'

Ambition and desire marched hand in hand in this determined young woman, Carenza saw. She wanted the accolade of being Gareth Llewellyn's partner on stage. She wanted him for herself in real life. The two went together.

And who was Carenza to stand in her way? A no one. A girl he had looked at with brief glimmerings of desire, once or twice, who would be instantly forgotten once the world that was rightfully his reclaimed him.

She knew it was quite irrational, because her being invited here at all had initially been only a titbit to make her happy—and then, of course, she had proved herself useful by deputising for Mrs Williams with the catering. All the same, what Marianne had told her—and the plain hint given out by Beth that she was the pretender to the crown, both personally and professionally—took the gloss off the afternoon for her.

The mention of Celia seemed to have cast a cloud over the rest of the party, too. Some of their natural effervescence was dampened, and the atmosphere was more subdued. Still, they lingered a while longer, and it was after four before Beth made the decision to set off back to Birmingham where the Shakespeare Trust was based.

'I prefer to drive those mountain roads in daylight,' she said. 'But thank you for inviting us, Gareth, and for giving us such a lovely afternoon. You too, Carenza,' she added with a warm smile. 'The food was fantastic, and it was nice meeting you.'

Carenza could not stifle a blush of pleasure. 'You're more than welcome. I shall be able to name-drop to all my friends in the Spotlight Players for months to come!' she laughed.

Marianne clearly did not care for Carenza's sharing the thanks as co-hostess, rather than just another guest. She reached up on tiptoes and kissed Gareth on the mouth, and, although she kept it light, somehow she managed to infuse it with a world of sensual promise.

'Don't leave it too long before you come back to us,' she urged. '"'If it were done when 'tis done, then 'twere well it were done quickly.'"'

Oh, clever, Carenza thought. She could imagine Marianne making an excellent scheming, ambitious Lady Macbeth!

After the Mercedes had vanished from sight, Carenza and Gareth turned instinctively to look at each other. His eyebrows were raised in a question, and she was seized by a sudden shyness.

'Thank you so much for inviting me, too,' she said. 'I really enjoyed meeting them.'

'No thanks necessary. You did all the work,' he pointed out. 'But I think now they've been down here and seen that I really am back in the land of the living they're reassured about my intentions of getting back to work.'

More than that, Carenza thought, Marianne was set and determined on becoming the next acting Mrs Llewellyn. She turned away from him, wishing it could be as easy to turn her back on this uncomfortable possibility, and retraced her steps into the living-room where she began stacking and clearing plates.

'Hey!' he protested. 'What do you think you're doing?'

'We can't leave all this for poor Mrs Williams,' she said. 'Besides, if her kids are ill she may not be back for some time. It won't take long to put this lot in the dishwasher and set the programme.'

'Then let me help. You've done enough,' he insisted firmly.

Together they cleared away the dishes and what little remained of the food. Carenza concentrated on the practicalities, trying *not* to be conscious of Gareth's nearness, but it was impossible to be so close and be unaware of him. The accidental brush of his arm against hers sent a wild tingling up her spine, and, if an unintentional contact like that could affect her so strongly, how, she wondered, would she feel if he *really* touched her?

All afternoon, she had been busy playing a part, that of casual friend and theatrical afficionado, desperately concealing from him, and from everyone else, the fact that she had stupidly and unexpectedly fallen in love with this man. It was a role which did not come easily to her, for her eyes were drawn to him wherever he happened to be, her senses were attuned to him, and responded crazily whenever he came near her, she thrilled to the sound of his voice, was suffused with pleasure and consternation when she felt his eyes on her.

And now they were alone it was a hundred times worse. Something had happened to her which she had carefully and consciously avoided all her life, but in spite of all her mental precautions it had still happened. The force was too strong to resist, and she, when it came to it, was as weak and helpless to fight against it as anyone else.

'Now that's out of the way we can relax,' said Gareth. Picking up the remains of a bottle of white wine and two clean glasses, he strolled out into the garden and sat down on the grass. Leaning back easily on one elbow, he filled both glasses. 'Come on—let's have a quiet drink.'

Carenza sat primly at his side, clutching her glass. The heat of the day had scarcely faded, but she was shivering so fiercely that she was sure he must be aware of it. Because this strange, incomprehensible business of being in love brought not only an idealised adoration of the loved one—it also involved desire, and this was an uneasy, complex, untried emotion to her. She wanted—needed—him to touch her, and was at the same time terrified out of her senses by the ferocity of that need.

Steady on, she told herself firmly. He doesn't know how you feel, and he doesn't feel that way about you. Keep calm, be friendly, be normal. A man and a girl enjoying a drink together on a summer's day, that's all. At any moment, you can get up and leave, so why don't you?

Because I can't, she answered herself readily enough. Because I don't know when, if ever again, I will be alone with him. Maybe never. Perhaps never again will I be close enough to watch how his mouth curves at the corners, how his hair grows back from his forehead, springing strongly from the roots. Never again to hear his voice speaking low and soft and only to me. If this afternoon is all I am to have, how can I run away from it—even though this feeling scares me witless?

He drained his glass and set it down, his eyes resting on her, sober and thoughtful.

'I should go,' she said half-heartedly.

'Not yet,' he said softly. 'Stay, Carenza. Carenza...'

All around them, the solitude of the hot afternoon stretched away to infinity. Apart from birdsong, there was no sound, and they were totally alone together in this small paradise. The drowsy hush of high summer enclosed them, wrapped around them, and Carenza felt her control slipping away, under its hypnotic spell.

She watched, unable to move, as he slowly raised a hand and, very gently, with just his forefinger, drew a line across her forehead. It moved lingeringly down, across her cheekbone, and traced the line of her jaw before he ran it lightly along her lower lip. And now she was trembling fiercely, unable to hide from him the obvious truth that his touch affected her deeply.

'Gareth...' she whispered in a faint, alarmed protestation, knowing herself for a hypocrite, for she did not want him to stop.

'Carenza...' His caressing finger slid down the long incline of her neck to where the pulse beat at the base of her throat. 'Ah—you do things to me...it's so long since I felt...it's like coming back to life,' he murmured in a low voice. And then, in one swift, but leisurely action, he had risen up on both knees, and his mouth followed the path his hand had taken, lightly kissing her brow, her cheek, and finally coming to rest, with a long, slow shudder of release, on her mouth.

A little cry welled up in her throat, but she did not resist as he lowered her to the grass and continued kissing her, more strongly, more deeply, unmistakably in earnest, and now she was free to do what she had ached to do—to run her own hands through his hair, to explore the muscles of his back with wondering fingers, new and untasted delights she had never known or wanted until she met him.

Still kissing her, he unfastened the buttons of her sundress, one by one. It was so hot that she had not worn a bra, and even as he unpeeled her, like a ripe fruit, the thought flitted across her mind that it looked for all the world as if she had come prepared for seduction. But she had not; how could she have envisaged a situation like this? Then the thought was gone, all thought was banished as she looked down on his bent dark head, overcome by a longing to surrender completely to the intensity of pleasure and desire his mouth was arousing in her.

But she couldn't . . . she dared not allow this to go further, for this way lay hurt and betrayal and unhappiness. He wanted her now, but tomorrow . . . and the next day . . . and when he was back in his real world, with the stage, and . . . and Marianne . . .

'Gareth, stop . . . I don't . . .' she began urgently. He paused only to raise his head, encircling her with one arm while his free hand explored her body, awakening more areas of response than she had believed existed.

'Carenza, my sweet, you do . . . look at you, you want to make love as much as I do . . .' he said, looking down intently and persuasively into her eyes.

'But . . . but . . . out here, in the open air, it's indecent . . .' she stammered idiotically, and he laughed, a low, sensual chuckle.

'No one can see us. There's no one for miles around,' he reassured her, his hand sliding down her thigh, touching her until she was in a frenzy of mingled desire and panic. 'But if you would prefer it I'll take you properly into the bedroom and shut the curtains. It would be a shame, though. You're very lovely to look at. The pleasure is visual as well as tactile.'

And that was all it was. Pleasure. He would make love to her out of his re-awakening response to all the stimuli of life; she would be a symbol of his re-entry into the world, but that was all. He did not, could not love her. Celia was still enthroned in his heart, and would remain there until someone like Marianne finally usurped her place. She, Carenza, would be no more than an interlude between two acts.

'I don't want to make love, here, or in the bedroom, or anywhere else!' she cried, putting both hands against his chest and pushing hard. She expected resistance. He was at least as aroused as she, vastly more experienced, and probably well aware of the effect he had on women. But, to her surprise, he released her easily, spreading out his hands in a gesture which indicated that she was free to go.

'Obviously, I got the wrong idea,' he said drily, with just a touch of contempt lurking in his voice. 'All the lights seemed to be on green. You come here half naked under your dress, and every time we touch I feel a thousand volts ignite between us.

It never occurred to me that you were in the teasing business.'

She fumbled wretchedly with the buttons of her dress, avoiding the scorn she guessed she would see in his eyes.

'I'm not a tease,' she said miserably. 'The truth is, I haven't . . . I mean, I never . . .'

She faltered, unable to finish, and, at last daring to look at him, she saw an expression of puzzled comprehension on his face.

'Are you trying to tell me that you're a virgin?' he asked bluntly.

She nodded mutely, and he gave a heavy sigh.

'Oh, lord, Carenza, I never thought,' he said ruefully. 'You seemed to have so much potential passion in you . . . and you're what? Twenty-three or so?'

'Twenty-four,' she admitted almost apologetically, as if confessing to a crime. 'All right, so it's unusual nowadays, but I never met anyone I wanted to . . . to . . .'

'You surprise me.' His tone was dry. 'It's a natural drive, after all. One doesn't have to be head over heels in love . . . curiosity is usually enough motivation to begin with. After that, mutual attraction will take one a long way.'

Drive . . . motivation . . . curiosity . . . attraction . . . the very words he used made it clear to her that he was light years away from the feelings which had coursed through her when he held her in his arms. Suddenly she was very angry, and very bitter. What did he take her for? Someone to call on when he needed an emergency catering service? And, having made use of her in that connection, and given her the chance to meet famous actors who would not normally come her way, he no doubt thought that it would amuse him, and round off her afternoon, if he made a little casual love to her. Perhaps he thought that was what she had really come for? That she would find a tumble in the grass with the great Gareth Llewellyn a memorable experience?

'Well, obviously it didn't take me far enough!' she stated bitingly. 'I'm sorry if I gave you the impression I'd be an easy lay, and then turned out to be a disappointment. It won't happen again, I can assure you!'

She had jumped to her feet, hands clenched angrily at her side, and he uncoiled and stood up with leisurely indifference, looking at her with a cool, measured scorn.

'Much ado about nothing!' he said coldly, cuttingly. 'You can be certain it won't happen again! I may have led a celibate life, of late, but I haven't reached a point of desperation where I need to seduce frustrated virgins.'

*Frustrated* virgins? Carenza glared at him, fury replacing hurt in her expressive brown eyes.

'How dare you?' she exclaimed, shaking with rage and humiliation. 'Let me tell you this, Mr High and Mighty Gareth Llewellyn—you may be God's gift to the theatre—you may also be God's gift to women, and I don't deny I am nobody important. But I am a human being, and it's my business who I make love to, and when, *if at all*.'

He looked at her as if he was genuinely puzzled by her words. 'I never heard so much over-excited nonsense,' he said contemptuously. 'Who I am, who you are, has nothing at all to do with it. We are...were...simply a man and a woman who were attracted to one another. Or so I thought. Now you're telling me otherwise, although, frankly, I find it hard to believe.'

Carenza blushed furiously. Minutes ago, she had been half naked in his arms, and her pleasure at his touch had been unmistakable and impossible to hide.

'If you got the wrong idea, I'm sorry,' she said, as coldly and firmly as possible. 'I must have had too much wine to drink, and, for a moment, got carried away. That's all there was to it.'

She picked up her handbag, nervously brushing back her disordered hair with one hand.

'And now I think I had better go,' she declared forcefully.

The contempt in his eyes shaded to a scornful amusement. 'Why?' he demanded softly. 'Are you afraid of what might happen if you stayed? There's no need to be, you know. I'm too old and tired a hand to play that sort of adolescent game. Quite frankly, I don't have the heart for it. I thought you were a mature woman who knew what she wanted.'

'No, I'm not a theatrical sophisticate who jumps blithely from bed to bed,' she retorted sarcastically. 'Just a plain, ordinary schoolteacher. And right now what I want more than anything is to get out from here!'

She turned and practically ran through the conservatory, across the enormous drawing-room, and down the corridor to the front door, which fortunately still stood open, since she was in no state to fumble with its ornate old locks. She was wrenching open the door of her car before the sound of his voice made her aware that he had followed her.

He stood in the doorway, looking quite calm and untroubled now—and why shouldn't he? she thought wretchedly. All he had lost out on was a brief sexual encounter which had not meant that much to him. And, as she stared resentfully at him, without visibly altering his stance, he slipped into the character of Othello, assuming a towering, tragic self-confidence.

'"Soft you—a word or two before you go——"'

Carenza shook her head fiercely. 'Stop it, Gareth! I don't want to play games, either!'

'Very well.' He let it go again, as easily as shrugging off a robe, and, even now, she had to marvel at the brilliant simplicity of his genius. 'I don't suppose you're in the mood to accept advice from me, but I'll tell you just one thing. From the little I've seen of your acting, I can deduce that you're good. I haven't seen sufficient to know *how* good, but I suspect the potential is there.'

'Am I supposed to be flattered, or mollified, by that?' she asked warily.

'No,' he said bluntly. 'You're supposed to take note that any creative artist learns by living. There is a whole range of emotions you will find it hard to simulate on stage, unless you have at least an inkling of them in real life. Open up. Experience. Otherwise, it's a leap you may never make.'

Now it was her turn to display contempt. 'Oh, that's excellent!' she exclaimed. 'In other words, sleeping with you would help me to turn in a better performance as Desdemona? Nice one, Gareth!'

He shrugged, a gesture of supreme indifference. 'I did not say it had to be me. In fact,' he said thoughtfully, a shadow of a smile creasing his mouth, 'in fact, it had better not be me. You're too naïve, too inexperienced, and altogether too pure. I'd be bad for you. Go away and find yourself a nice man, somewhere. You might surprise yourself.'

'Oh——!' An exclamation of impotent fury escaped her as she slid swiftly into the car, slammed the door and started the engine.

All the way back to the farmhouse her anger seethed inside her as she drove, and, fortunately for her, the roads were relatively quiet, with little traffic.

Of all the arrogant, conceited, self-centred…she thought explosively, turning off down the narrow lanes towards the farm, braking quickly to avoid a flock of chickens. What had he called her? A frustrated virgin! A tease. Naïve, inexperienced, needing the sexual attentions of a man to release her! How dared he? How *dared* he!

There was no sign of Sammy back at the caravan. The day had been so glorious that obviously the picnic had extended itself into a swimming session. Carenza kicked off her sandals and flung herself into the window-seat, gazing glumly across the bay at Holyhead mountain, outlined against a sky still resolutely blue.

Beneath her surface outrage, an honest little voice kept on nagging—wasn't Gareth perhaps just a tiny bit right? How many twenty-four-year-old women were there, these days, who hadn't at least tested the water, if not plunged right in? And so long as she consistently kept herself hermetically sealed from all intimate sexual contact how could she hope to understand the emotions of the heroines she portrayed?

But I'm beginning, she thought miserably. The leap of her heart as she caught sight of Gareth across a room, the memory of how she had almost burst into flame at the touch of his hands on her skin—oh, yes, she knew why Desdemona would have swum the ocean from Venice to Cyprus to be with Othello.

In spite of the angry words she had flung at Gareth, the burning, humiliating resentment, the bitterness still raging within her, nothing had changed, or could change the hopeless love for him that had so suddenly and so completely taken hold of her. She would walk barefoot across fire for him, were he to hold out his hand—even now.

But he didn't want her. Not in the way that she wanted him. All he had wanted was an hour's amusement on a summer afternoon, to convince himself that for all he had suffered and lost the woman he loved he was still a man... still capable of feeling the need to make love to a woman.

For just those few hours, today, she had aroused his desire, but she had proved unable to satisfy it. Now, even if she were to go back to him and say, I'm here, take me, she knew he would turn her away. A fearful virgin was one problem too many for Gareth Llewellyn, as he took his first step back towards the life he had left behind.

'I'd be bad for you. Go away and find yourself a nice man,' he had urged her.

There's no other man for me, my love, she thought sorrowfully. The curtain falls—almost before it has risen.

## CHAPTER SEVEN

IT WASN'T until a few days later that Carenza discovered that she had mislaid her locket. It was a slim golden one on a chain, which the other students at drama school had given her when she was reluctantly obliged to leave, and although it was not terribly valuable she had a sentimental attachment to it. She did not wear it often, and so she could not at first remember where she had lost it, and she searched the caravan and all around in an attempt to find it.

'You had it when you went to lunch with Gorgeous Gareth,' Sammy informed her.

'Are you sure?' Carenza asked doubtfully. 'And please stop referring to him in that way.'

'Well, he is! And yes, I'm sure,' her sister said. 'You were wearing your print sundress, white sandals, your jet earrings, and the locket.'

For a moment, Carenza had a visual flashback of Gareth's strong brown hands unfastening her dress, his dark head bent to her breasts. She had no recollection of his fingers catching on the locket—his hands had known very well where they were going—and the memory of how exposed and vulnerable she had felt convinced her that she had been wearing nothing above the waist, not even a chain.

'I don't think so,' she said, turning away so that Sammy would not see the red flush that crept

115

shamefully up her neck. 'I must have lost it some-where else.'

'Have it your way,' Sammy shrugged. 'You can always ask him when you see him if it's turned up somewhere at Plas Gwyn.'

'I don't think I shall be seeing him again,' she replied quickly. 'I told you—it was just a one-off thing. Gareth will be returning to the theatre, soon. He'll be too busy to bother with casual acquaintances.'

'What a shame! He really *is* gorgeous! And nice, too. I didn't think famous people could be nice,' Sammy sighed. 'Here I was, thinking we'd got you all fixed up!'

'Don't be silly!' Carenza snapped, more sharply than she had intended. She forbore to add that Gareth Llewellyn was far from being 'nice' much of the time. He was caustic, scornful and ruthlessly critical.

Both Sammy and Bronwen had been curious about her afternoon at the Llewellyn house, and it was fortunate that by the time she had had to face either of them Carenza had pulled herself together.

Yes, she had said, she had had an enjoyable day. She had talked a lot about the house, a lot about the people she had met, and said as little as poss-ible about Gareth himself. It would not do to give either of those two the remotest suspicion that there was anything at all going on between Gareth and herself, and so she had deliberately kept her ac-count cool and amusing and dispassionate. She was doing more acting in her own life than she was on stage, lately, she thought wryly.

Of course, she saw nothing of Gareth himself over the next few days, nor did she expect to. Their brief association had come to an end in the moment when, for him, it had crystallised into desire which she had failed to satisfy. She was not too innocent to know that to most men virgins spelled trouble. They could not stand the pace; they were nervous and made awkward demands. Even without that final rancorous argument she doubted she would have heard any more from him. So she had been stupid enough to fall in love—that was *her* problem.

And then, one night as she was in the shower, it came to her where she had last seen the locket. Before Marianne St John and the others arrived, she had been upstairs, washing her face in the bathroom at Plas Gwyn. It had been in that stunned moment when she had realised that what she felt for Gareth wasn't mere attraction or hero-worship, but love. Her hands had been all atremble, and she had removed the locket because it had become tangled in her hair as she brushed it. She had been in such a flustered state that she must have forgotten to put it on again.

But she must have been up there again during the afternoon—how come she had not seen it, or no one else had remarked on it? And surely, if he had come across it, Gareth would have realised whose it was, since it had Sammy's photo inside. He could have posted it on to her, even if he had no wish to see her again.

It was a mystery to Carenza, and one she had no means of solving. In no circumstances dared she return to Plas Gwyn—certainly not under the pretext of searching for a piece of jewellery which she was not sure she would find where she believed she had left it. She could not even summon the nerve to phone him and ask. He would only think she had had second thoughts and was now chasing him, panting to continue where they had left off.

The only thing she could do was to wait until a reasonable time had elapsed, then write a cool little note asking if the locket had by any chance been found there. If she wrote from Longbridge even his infernal conceit could not lead him to suspect she was itching for his attentions.

And was she? There were times when Carenza awoke in the night to a profound restlessness, and before the barriers of consciousness had time to spring up and protect her she imagined that Gareth was kissing her, his mouth hard and sweetly relentless on hers, that his wonderfully expert hands were caressing her body, until she groaned and ached, wanting him to finish what he had begun.

Somewhere beyond the excitement and pleasure, thrilling as they were in themselves, must lie the immense, immeasurable experience of loving and being loved—of two people so closely meshed that they no longer knew where one identity ended and the other began. The supreme trust of knowing that someone was there for you, always, no matter what, caring, trusting, understanding——

But stop! It wasn't like that. Didn't she know it wasn't? Beyond that beautiful illusion lurked the inevitable pain and disillusionment when the dream ended. Had she forgotten how it had been when her father left?

She'd risk it, Carenza thought soberly in the still darkness of the night, astonishing herself by the thought. If Gareth loved her, she would take the chance; she would put herself out on a limb, chancing the future pain for the miracle of having his love, even for a short time.

And what of Gareth, who knew at first hand how it felt to be hurt and betrayed? Perhaps one day even he would take the gamble on finding happiness again with someone else. But since she would not be the one it was both pointless and painful to dwell on it.

'I think it's about time we went back to Longbridge,' she said at breakfast, after one such night, when neither her heart nor her body could find any peace.

'But there's heaps of holiday left!' Sammy exclaimed, dismayed.

'School holidays, yes. But most of the Spotlight group will be back from wherever they've been, and we really do have lots of work to do on the play.'

She was amazed when her sister, after staring blankly at her for a few seconds, jumped up, burst into tears, and ran out, leaving the caravan door swinging behind her.

Carenza searched everywhere around for Sammy, and, failing to find her, went across to the farmhouse to seek advice from Bronwen.

'She just belted off,' she said, nursing her mug of steaming-hot tea. 'I don't know where she's gone, although I know she can't be far away, and she knows the area so well that she's unlikely to come to any real harm. What worries me is that her behaviour was so unlike Sammy!'

Bronwen pushed the sugar across the table towards her. 'Were you never a teenage girl?' she asked with a smile.

'Well, yes,' Carenza frowned. 'Of course I was. Although to be honest I didn't have a lot of time to savour the experience. Mum wasn't coping too well, and...' She spooned sugar absently into her tea, stirring with unnecessary vigour.

Bronwen patted her hand. 'Sammy is perfectly normal for her age, I promise you,' she said. 'I'll send Trefor to find her, in a minute. He'll know where to look, most likely.'

'Trefor?' Carenza looked up, alerted by something knowing in Bronwen's voice.

'Oh, come on, Carenza! You must have noticed how much time they spend together? Don't you know your sister and my son have a...a fondness for one another?'

'But...but she's only fourteen!' Carenza spluttered into her tea.

'So was Juliet when she and Romeo got into such hot water,' Bronwen laughed. 'You see—I do know a little about Shakespeare. Not that I'm suggesting things between Trefor and Sammy are at that level!'

Carenza heaved a deep sigh, and shook her head. No wonder Sammy had been keener than ever to come down, this year. However didn't I notice that the poor kid was in the throes of first love? she wondered, and then immediately answered herself— because I was so tied up with my own feelings about Gareth that I failed to take note of what was in front of my eyes. And Sammy—she hadn't said a word, but if she was half as confused as Carenza herself she probably didn't know what was happening to her.

'Wow!' she said. 'Aren't I the prize idiot?'

'Look you,' Bronwen said easily, 'if you feel you must get back it will be fine to leave Sammy here with us. She can bunk in with Joanna. And you needn't worry about her and Trefor—he knows she's only young, and, although he's keen, he's treating her like cut glass. Besides, he knows if there were any hanky-panky Dai would be down on him like a ton of cement.'

Carenza walked slowly back to the caravan, full of the astounding, slightly painful realisation that her kid sister was growing up. Maybe this, with Trefor, was only a boy-girl thing that would not outlast the summer, but it had begun. Little Sam had started to become a woman.

When Sammy finally turned up, looking quiet and chastened, Carenza only smiled gently and said, 'There's no need for you to come back to Longbridge with me. Bronwen has very kindly said you can stay with them, and I'll come down later to fetch you.'

Her sister's eyes exploded with stars. 'Terrific!' she breathed, and then, as a concerned afterthought, 'Shall you be all right on your own?'

'I'll be fine,' Carenza assured her. 'I've lots to do—preparation for school, and rehearsals for the play. Don't worry about me. Just have fun.'

She didn't press Sammy to tell her anything about Trefor. Her sister would do that in her own good time, and maybe, as yet, she wasn't even aware that there was anything to tell.

But for herself, for the first time ever, she knew she would be glad to get away from Anglesey. Just knowing that Gareth was here, and that she would not see him—that he had no further desire to see her—was torture she could do without. Not that she fooled herself distance would lessen her obsession with him, but it would put him physically out of her way, beyond her reach. She had to start forgetting him, and get her life back on the calm, even, unexciting lines on which it had run before she knew him.

It was rather like reorganising a city after it had been stricken by a major earthquake, she realised once she was back in Longbridge. She pottered aimlessly around the flat, which was absurdly quiet without Sammy, shopped, cooked—and how boring cooking for one could be—made a start on some of the work she had to do in readiness for the start of the new school year in September. All the familiar parameters were there, yet nothing was the same.

It was she who had changed, Carenza knew. How could she ever have imagined she could go back to the way she had once been—calm, quiet, untouched by storms of emotion? Would her life ever be that simple, that straightforward again, or did she have to carry around with her forever the burden of this love she could neither fulfil nor be free of?

A few days after her return the Spotlight Players were due to meet for their regular evening rehearsal, but just as Carenza was finishing her solitary dinner she had a frantic phone call from Briony.

'Thank heavens you're back!' she said fervently. 'The most awful thing has happened, although in view of what I told you before I can't say I'm surprised. Lynne and Perry have split up—separated!'

'Oh, no!' Carenza groaned. She had been hoping Perry's differences with his wife were no more than a temporary setback, and that after their holiday the couple would be able to restore their relationship. 'Is there any hope of their getting back together...? I mean, is it permanent?'

'According to Lynne it is,' Briony said glumly. 'She was in the office today, but only to clear her desk, and now she's taken indefinite leave. Perry has moved out of the house altogether, she says, and gone to stay with his parents in London. He won't be back until school re-opens.'

At first, all Carenza's thoughts were concentrated on the awful personal dilemma which had struck her friend and colleague. Only as she absorbed the full implications did another aspect occur to her.

'But Briony—the play!' she said, horrified. 'What are we going to do?'

'There's nothing we can do. We don't have a director,' Briony said bluntly. 'Perry was the guiding force, and there's no one else willing, let alone able, to take over. We'll just have to fold—for the moment, anyhow. *Othello* was struggling, anyway, you've got to admit.'

'Hold on!' Suddenly Carenza was reluctant to give up all they had worked so hard to achieve. 'We can't just let it all go! We had problems, yes, but they could be worked out. If we cancel *Othello* it could be the beginning of the end for the Spotlight

Players. We'll just fall apart. But if we keep going, somehow... well, I'm sure Perry will come back, eventually. If his marriage is really breaking up, he's going to need us, need *something* to keep him going.'

'All that may well be true, but who's going to direct *Othello*, Carenza?' Briony demanded worriedly. 'Can *you* do it—as well as playing Desdemona?'

Carenza blanched. She had never directed before, and although her own part was beginning to take shape more clearly in her mind she had no idea whether she had the managerial and inspirational qualities, the sheer authority required to show others the way, to pull the whole together and breathe life into it.

Nevertheless, she said recklessly, 'I'd give it a go, rather than see the whole thing collapse and vanish down the drain! Let's talk about it tonight, when we're all together, and see if we can't work something out.'

Too agitated now to concentrate on anything else, she slipped on comfortable shoes and went for a walk in the park. The evening was still fine and sunny; the park was full of children on holiday from school, and there were people playing tennis on the municipal courts, strolling along the paths, or just lying on the grass, luxuriating in the warmth.

Carenza observed all this, but only with half her mind. She was thinking about that day at Plas Gwyn, and how she had talked with such enthusiasm about the play with Beth, Mel and Cyril. Although they were true professionals, and she was only an amateur, she had felt that she shared with them a dream that only those who loved the theatre could fully understand. Gareth shared it too, so fiercely that it was drawing him back, in spite of his long resistance, and Carenza could not escape the feeling that if she gave up on *Othello* and the Spotlight Players now she would somehow break the tentative thread which linked her to him, however loosely.

It would be as if it had never happened. As if she had never known him, talked with him, shared that strong communion of ideas that came from loving and caring about the same things. As if he had never held her in his arms and made her thrill to his touch. They might have parted with angry words, he might have made it clear there was no part in his life for her, but she could not regret their meeting—not now, not ever. And all she had left of it, a kind of bitter legacy, was *Othello*.

Inspired with a nervous determination, she walked more briskly back to the flat, ready to go and fight for what she believed they should do. Bursting into the lobby and heading for the stairs, she was totally unprepared for the voice that arrested her.

'Carenza! I was beginning to think I had wasted my time, coming here.'

'Gareth!' Her breath escaped her in a stifled gasp; she stood stock-still, incredulous, as he uncoiled himself with unhurried but agile grace from the seat in the communal entrance hall. Her stomach churned painfully, and that strange, not to be forgotten trembling started up once again, draining the strength from her legs. And yet her heart was alive and singing with joy at the sight of him.

'What on earth are you doing here?' she asked with forced coolness. Try to remember the names he called you that day at Plas Gwyn, the harsh, sarcastic things he said, the disdain in his eyes. Don't look at him, standing there, close enough to reach out and touch, his black cords and white sweatshirt emphasising the tan of his arms and face, that deep, world-weary smile, the brilliant eyes...

'I came to return this...' He reached into the pocket of his trousers and drew out Carenza's locket on its thin gold chain. 'It must have slipped on to the bathroom floor, and Mrs Williams found it when she came back on duty and gave the place a good clean. I knew it had to be yours, since it has your sister's picture inside.'

And it isn't the sort of high-class jewellery Beth or Marianne would wear, Carenza thought. She still had not moved.

'Don't you want it back?'

He dangled it tantalisingly in front of her, and, as if she were an automaton, Carenza held out her hand. He dropped it into her palm, and then, surprisingly, closed her fingers over it with his own strong, warm ones. She could not draw her hand away, for all she knew she should, and it was he who broke the contact.

'How...how did you find me?'

'How do you think? I went to the Pritchard farmhouse to ask for your address, and found your sister there. We had quite a chat.'

'You did?' Carenza's voice was faint with suppressed apprehension, praying that Sammy had guessed nothing of how she really felt about Gareth. She wouldn't put it past her sister to stir a little.

'Mm.' He dug both hands back in his pockets and regarded her long and thoughtfully, his eyes making a careful and unrevealing inspection that left her weak. 'She told me all about your mother dying, and how you brought her up. I remember your saying your father had deserted you, but I assumed you had other relatives. I didn't realise you and she were alone in the world.'

She shrugged. Trust Sammy—doubtless she had laid on the pathos with a trowel!

'Sammy and I have lived this way for some years. We're used to it,' she said tersely. 'Does it matter, Gareth?'

'I think it does,' he said evenly. 'You've made yourself into a fortress, Carenza. A four-gated barbican with lookouts posted and portcullis firmly lowered.'

The symbolism was unmistakable, and Carenza flushed angrily.

'It's none of your business. You didn't like it when I tried to tell *you* how to run your life,' she pointed out.

'No more I did, but what you said got through to me, and I took action. I'm only returning the favour.'

She turned swiftly, at last released from the gripping paralysis he had induced in her. 'Well, don't! I don't need your advice.'

He was quicker, his hand grasping her wrist and holding it firmly. 'I let you into my home, if reluctantly at first,' he said quietly, but in a voice that did not admit refusal. 'Aren't you going to invite me into yours?'

'All right. But I'm going out soon,' she said grudgingly, wondering how she could bear to be near him for longer than five minutes without wanting him to kiss her.

He released her arm and she led the way upstairs, unlocking the door to her flat, glad that it was at least tidy, but wishing it were less bland, more characterful. But he strolled casually over to the window and remarked on how fortunate she was to have such a pleasant view of the park, and, his eyes seeking out the shelf where she kept her accumulated souvenirs, added, 'Ah—there's the elephant.'

Carenza swallowed hard. She remembered all too well the day they had bought him. Gareth and herself in the market at Llangefni—''For the lady who cooks a mean breakfast''. And in the pub, his eyes looking deep into hers, his touch . . . Why did she have to keep harping back to that?

'Would you . . . would you like a drink?' she asked. Anything to keep her occupied, she thought grimly, as she mixed the gin and tonic he asked for and poured herself a rather too liberal glass of wine.

'It was good of you to bring the locket, but you could have left it with Sammy, or posted it,' she pointed out.

'I could,' he agreed. 'But I was coming over to Birmingham, anyway, so it's not out of my way. I've just sold the house Celia and I lived in, and bought a flat.'

His hesitation before her name was so slight, so fractional that a less interested ear might have missed it.

'But you're not going to sell Plas Gwyn?' she could not prevent herself from asking.

'No, I'm not.' A smile chased the shadow from his eyes. 'Despite what Marianne says, we *do* have time off, and Plas Gwyn is a good place to relax. It's odd—although I'm Welsh . . . that is to say, my parents were Welsh, obviously, with a name like Llewellyn—I've never lived in Wales until now, and it's made me appreciate my ancestry. I feel Welsh now. At Plas Gwyn, I am in touch with my roots.'

He looked down into his glass, and then back directly at Carenza.

'Marianne was right about one thing, though. Celia *would* have hated it. But——' again the hesitation '—Celia's gone. I'm alive. I've accepted that.'

But would Marianne like it? Carenza drew a deep breath. There was something she had to know, although she hardly dared ask.

'Gareth . . . were you happy . . . you and Celia?'

He set his glass down heavily on the table, and his eyes were hard, his voice sharp as he snapped, 'Why do you ask?'

She took a step back, involuntarily. 'I . . . I don't know,' she faltered defensively. 'It just seems to me that so many marriages flounder, so many people are unhappy in them. Is it inevitable?'

He shrugged. 'If you're looking for a fail-safe recipe, I don't have one. Celia was no saint, nor am I.' He finished his drink. 'You said you were going out, so I'll be on my way.'

He had not answered her question, but she had not really expected him to. Still, there had been a subtle shift in his attitude from the way he had spoken about Celia the first time Carenza had insinuated herself into Plas Gwyn. Then it had been as if his dead wife were still . . . enshrined, yes, that was exactly the word . . . enshrined in his memory. Now, an unmistakable note of cynicism had crept in. He knew—just as Marianne had said, and perhaps, to himself at least, he had admitted it. She thought that was probably more painful than the comforting blanket of illusion he had discarded.

Nervously, she picked up her books and script, and, noting them, he said, 'Why didn't you tell me I was keeping you from rehearsal?'

Carenza sighed. 'Because you aren't. Not really,' she said, a wave of relief seizing her as she unburdened herself to the one person she knew who, whatever else he might think of her, would understand.

'Tell me.' It was a command, not a request. He perched on the edge of the table, arms folded, waiting, and she complied with a willing obedience which amazed her.

'We've lost our director—another one with marriage problems. He's temporarily left town, and no one else in the cast wants the responsibility,' she told him. 'Unless I'm prepared to take it on myself, the production will fold . . . and I think our dramatic society will probably break up.'

'*You?*' He looked hard at her, and gave a short laugh. 'I'm sorry if I sound derogatory, but acting and directing at the same time is a formidable task, and your performance will suffer if you attempt to do both.'

'I won't have a performance—we won't have a play—unless I do!' she retorted, stung by his doubts, but aware that they only echoed her own.

'Everyone else clearly shares your unbounded confidence in my ability, so unless I can talk them round, it's all over. Finished.'

He stood up. 'Come along,' he said briskly. 'Get your things together and let's go.'

She gaped at him. 'Go where?'

'I'm coming with you. To talk to your cast—see if I can whip up some enthusiasm,' he said gravely.

*'You?'* Her voice assumed deliberately the exact pitch and inflexion of his, and his face broke into an appreciative grin.

'Well, why not? I'm not doing anything tonight. And I owe you one,' he added seriously.

She still stood there, in the middle of the room, staring at him in disbelief. He opened the door and held it open, anticipating her compliance as though he had no doubt it would be forthcoming.

'What are we waiting for?' said Gareth Llewellyn.

The Spotlight Players were momentarily dumbfounded when their leading lady turned up with a celebrity in tow, but they quickly recovered, and were not slow to bombard their distinguished guest with questions about his career, and theatrical matters in general. He took all this attention pleasantly and patiently, but after a while he held up his hand authoritatively and said, 'Enough about me. I'm resting, at the moment. You people have a play to put on.'

'No we don't,' Briony said gloomily. 'Didn't Carenza tell you—we don't have a director? There isn't one of us can do what Perry did.'

Gareth turned his powerhouse of a smile on her, and allowed its beam to embrace all of them. Even

Carenza, who was all too familiar with the charismatic force of his charm, when he chose to exert it, felt its warmth and its strength.

'Will you do something for me? Will you run through a scene...just one? Let's say, Act III Scene II, in which all the principals are involved. Let's see what you've got, before you talk about abandoning it.'

A whisper of nervous excitement ran through the hall, and a new tension, a vibrant alertness seemed to seize everyone. Apprehensive they might be, but no one was going to refuse this opportunity which they were sure would never come their way again. Places were taken swiftly and without demur. At the far side of the room, Gareth turned a chair the wrong way round and sat straddled across it, elbows leaning on its back, silently attentive, but, Carenza knew, missing nothing.

He let them run through to the end without interruption. At least, now, everyone knew their lines more or less, with only an odd word required now and then from Teresa, who prompted. It was far from perfect; it was also far from being a failure. Given that everyone was trying exceptionally hard to impress, but that they were all extremely nervous of their knowledgeable audience, there were moments when it leapt into life, when the spark caught and the characters lived, of their own volition. And as the scene came to an end a strong sense of anticlimax seized them all, and they stood sheepishly, waiting for a reaction.

Gareth rose and came down the aisle, smiling encouragingly.

'That wasn't half bad,' he said. 'But look, one or two things . . .' He leapt nimbly on to the stage. 'Othello—sorry, I've forgotten your name . . .'

'Nigel.'

'Nigel. You're beginning to suspect what Iago . . . Francis, is it? . . . has told you about your wife might be true. But you won't admit it readily. So when you say "'thinkest thou I'd make a life of jealousy?'" only the audience must catch the irony.'

For several minutes he moved swiftly about the stage, explaining, demonstrating, criticising, but not harshly; showing each of them how their performance could be subtly improved. So that when he said, 'Right, let's do it again,' no one hesitated, for all it was getting late. Each and every one of them felt the uplift he had given them, and came off stage with a warm sense of achievement.

'Better,' was all he said, but the one word was more valuable than a stream of more fulsome, less informed praise. 'You've worked hard—not only tonight, but for some time, I can tell. It would be a pity to throw all that away, don't you think?'

It was Francis who put into words what they were all thinking. 'We worked well tonight—because you helped us,' he said seriously. 'But much as we appreciate it, and enjoyed it, we know it won't be like that when we're left to our own devices. It will all disintegrate into chaos again. We *need* a director.'

Gareth stood up, and spread out his hands in a gesture Carenza found heartbreakingly familiar. His next words took her breath away.

'I agree,' he said simply. 'And now you have one. Me. Any objections?'

## CHAPTER EIGHT

GARETH and Carenza walked back through the warm summer night to where he had parked his car outside her flat. For a long time they walked in silence, until finally she asked simply, 'Why?'

'Several reasons,' he said. 'First of all, as I said, I owe you. You turned me round and pointed me in the right direction, and I'd like to repay the debt.'

'There's no debt,' Carenza insisted. The last thing she wanted was for him to feel beholden to her in any way.

'If you say so. Nevertheless.' They had reached the car park, and he jangled his car keys in his pocket. 'All right, then. Let's say I don't want to see a potentially good production go to waste. Let's say the theatre has given me so much that I'd be happy to give back a little, at grass roots level. Or I could be far less complicated and say simply that I'd enjoy the experience. Pick any of those explanations—or a combination of all of them.'

He paused.

'Don't you want me to direct you, Carenza? What's wrong? Are you fearful of the Desdemona I might draw out from you?'

If she had answered honestly, she would have said yes, but it was not the on-stage version of that passionate, sensual young woman she was afraid of, but the real live one, and her ability to draw a line between the two.

134

She said quietly, 'We said some pretty unpleasant things to each other at Plas Gwyn, that day, after we . . . after we got our wires crossed. I don't know if I can forget all that, when you are directing me.'

'You would have to if you were a professional actress,' he said shortly. 'Start thinking and behaving like a professional. You're good enough to be one, and, in fact, you should consider it.'

She sucked in her breath, and long, shining vistas of ambition she had turned her back on years ago briefly and seductively beckoned her. Then she shook her head.

'No, Gareth. It's too late now. My life is set in its course,' she said firmly.

'At twenty-four?' His incredulity was tinged with scorn. 'For heaven's sake, Carenza——' Then he seemed to collect himself deliberately. 'Well, that's up to you. My self-appointed task is to make you give the best Desdemona you're capable of, right now. And as for the other business . . .'

His lips compressed together in a firm, purposeful line, the brilliant grey eyes narrowed as he looked down at her.

'That's all behind us,' he said. 'There's no need for you to even think about it. After all, nothing very significant happened, did it? You left my house *virgo intacta*, which was what you wanted, and you needn't be afraid I shall be groping you behind the scenery. It's not my style. This will be a working relationship. All right?'

'Yes,' she said, in a tight little voice, shamed by his brisk dismissal of the events of that, to her, memorable afternoon. Nothing very significant had happened. She had only fallen in love. And for the first time ever she had wanted to make love, only she had been too scared and too conscious that he did not love her. But she had no other choice but to go along with his version.

She forced a light laugh. 'All right. What actress wouldn't give her eye-teeth to be directed by Gareth Llewellyn?' she demanded gaily. 'Now—can I offer you a cup of coffee before you set off back to Birmingham?'

He shook his head. 'Thank you, but no,' he said, and she could have sworn that there was a hint of amusement beneath the assumed gravity of his tone. 'I don't want you to start worrying that we might get our... wires crossed... again.'

A sense of outrage accompanied Carenza up to her flat, and she pulled the curtains closed with a vicious tug, refusing to look out and watch him drive away. What had he just been trying to tell her? That he thought she might lead him on and then refuse to deliver? That since he could not commit himself to loving a woman again he was only interested in relationships that included instant but casual sex? And, that being so, she was quite definitely off his list.

She compressed her lips firmly. He wanted a working relationship? Very well, that was precisely what he would get. No matter what it cost her, she would make very, very sure she never stepped over the thin line dividing the professional from the personal, nor gave him any inclination that she would like to do so.

She did not fool herself. Loving him as she did, it would be perhaps the hardest thing she had ever had to do. But he had made his position clear, and she would go along with it if it killed her, if only for the sake of her own self-respect. It was not much to cling to, but it was all she had.

And so began the strangest few weeks of Carenza's entire life, a brief space when Gareth Llewellyn took over her very being, reshaping her in a manner that was both frightening and exhilarating.

Twice a week he drove over from Birmingham to work with the Spotlight Players on their forthcoming production of *Othello*, which was scheduled to be performed in public at the beginning of September.

He made it very clear that the one condition he insisted upon was that his presence must be incognito, and his contribution unacknowledged.

'Your regular director did all the spadework. I'm just polishing up,' he said. 'I'm sure he will be back with you before too long, so his is the name which must go on all your publicity posters. Officially, I'm not here.'

'A pity—your name would certainly ensure that we received lots of attention,' Briony laughed.

'Yes—and some of it you wouldn't care for,' he told her soberly. 'I don't think having a coterie of the less scrupulous members of the Press camped outside the church hall, asking you inane questions and harassing you at every end and turn, would do wonders for your performance.'

'Modest, isn't he?' Nigel whispered, a trifle sarcastically in Carenza's ear.

'He's right, though,' she pointed out. 'If the Press got wind that Gareth was here, helping a

group of amateur actors put on a play, we'd be be-
sieged! None of us is used to dealing with that kind
of thing. And I don't think Gareth wants it himself,
at this point in time.'

Nigel looked peeved. 'You seem to know an awful
lot about his wants and needs,' he observed. 'You
haven't fallen for him, have you? That would be
foolish, Carenza. He's from another planet, and
he'll go back to it, once this is over.'

She kept her eyes and her voice steady. 'Thank
you for your concern—although it's really no one's
business but my own,' she said.

'Then why is he here?' Nigel persisted. 'We're
pretty small beer to someone like him. Is he just
amusing himself?'

'I don't think there's much point in analysing
Gareth's motives,' Carenza said evasively. 'He's
here—and we can only be thankful, and make the
most of it. All of us have learned—are learning—
a tremendous amount through working with him.'

'I'll give you that. He's a brilliant director,' Nigel
admitted. 'Hard, though. You can't get away with
anything less than your best.'

And that, she reflected, was certainly true. Cyril
Templeton had told her that Gareth was an utter
tyrant, and now she was finding it out for herself.
It wasn't that he shouted at them, or raged, or lost
his temper. He rarely raised his voice, and was, for
the most part, controlled and supremely patient.
But he would have it right, no matter what it took,
and when he spoke they listened. He gave and demanded total dedication, and the one thing that
made him angry was a failure to give it in return.

They learned very quickly that they could not get away with anything sloppy, shoddy, or ill thought out, but even then one scathing word of disapproval was enough to make the erring one thoroughly ashamed, because, above all, Gareth inspired. He made them want to give their all, to live up to the almost impossibly high standards he set. His incredible enthusiasm and energy coaxed from them qualities few of them knew they possessed.

Carenza went home from rehearsals at the same time elated and emotionally drained. Even as she lived and breathed her role, she was subconsciously aware of Gareth's all-seeing gaze fixed on her, and it seemed that on stage she gave herself to him completely as she could not do in reality. As she wanted to do, increasingly, every time she was with him. This intense, sublimated passion gave her portrayal a heightened sensitivity, and she felt herself soaring to new peaks. But when rehearsal was over she was once again Carenza Carlton, who loved a man she could not have, and who had to walk away with her lonely agony.

For Gareth never allowed their relationship to extend beyond the boundaries of the hall where they rehearsed. He said goodnight to her along with the rest of the cast, and drove back to Birmingham where, as she knew from the odd remarks he let slip, he was busy getting his new flat in order. That would be his base when he returned to the Shakespeare Trust, a symbol of his new life.

At weekends, she knew, he went to Anglesey, because Sammy told her so when she phoned.

'Gorgeous Gareth was here on Saturday,' she informed Carenza cheerfully.

Carenza had long since given up trying to correct this appellation.

'You saw him?' she asked cautiously.

'Sure. He came to see me, here at the farm. Joanna was gobsmacked.' She giggled. 'Bronwen made him a cup of tea, and he actually sat in the kitchen with us. He told me you were fine, and working very hard, and I wasn't to worry about you. Wasn't that nice of him to think about me?'

Yes, but Gareth Llewellyn never ceased to astound and puzzle Carenza. His motives and the workings of his mind were quite beyond her. He made it in his way to go to the Pritchard place to reassure Sammy about her, but off-stage she never got more from him than a cursory nod or a casual enquiry after her health.

'It was kind of you to look up Sammy,' she ventured to say to him when next they met. 'I'm sure she's just fine down there—Anglesey has always been *her* place—but we've never been separated this long.'

'Your sister is a very shrewd and capable young lady,' he said, regarding her with a cool, impersonal gaze. 'Her only worry is whether *you* are coping without *her*.'

His deliberately formal and distant manner stretched her carefully guarded control almost to breaking-point.

'I trust you set her mind at rest. I'm perfectly all right—never better,' she practically snapped at him.

'She seems to be of the opinion that you are alone too much,' he said coolly. 'She thinks you are in need of a companion of the...' his eyebrows rose in slight mockery '...of the opposite gender. Have you ever thought she may be right? Friend Nigel would appear to be thoroughly smitten with you.'

A humiliating rage began to boil up inside her. Not only had he made it abundantly clear he had no interest in her—he was trying to nudge her in the direction of someone else.

'This is supposed to be a working relationship, Gareth,' she remarked icily. 'That being so, I'd be thankful if you'd leave me to direct my own personal life! I don't interfere with yours.'

'That would be difficult, since you know next to nothing about my personal life,' he said loftily. 'You don't care much for the truth, do you? That quality which comes pouring out of you as Desdemona could use an outlet in reality.'

And that was too much! Despite the fact that they were taking a coffee break between scenes, with other people's conversations going on all around them, Carenza could not control her mortification nor her anger. Her hand came up, itching to slap his handsome, self-assured face, and she glared at him in wild frustration as he deflected her wrist, just in time.

'Not in public, my dear,' he said softly. 'I put one leading lady across my knee for that, and no one else is going to push me so far.'

And that, no doubt, must have been Celia Harman, Carenza thought bitterly, turning away, angry with him for so easily provoking then besting her, but even more angry with herself for losing her hard-won self-possession. He'd put Celia across his knee only because he'd loved her enough to let her arouse his emotions. But *she* did not have the power to do that.

After the next weekend, Sammy once more reported Gareth's presence on Anglesey.

'Don't tell me he came to the farm again?' Carenza asked, a touch sourly.

'No—not this time. Trefor and I went to Bull Bay, and we saw him walking on the beach with an absolutely stunning blonde girl,' Sammy said.

'I expect that would be Marianne St John,' Carenza replied, trying vainly to ignore the lead weight which had settled stubbornly where her heart was supposed to be. 'Did he see you?'

'Oh, yes. He introduced her, and that's who it was,' Sammy informed her. 'I'd never heard of her, but Bronwen said she's seen her on the telly. I didn't like her very much. She couldn't really be bothered with Trefor and me, and she made a snide remark about Gareth wasting his time and talent on some little amateur production.'

Carenza could well imagine Marianne's disapproval of Gareth's involvement with the Spotlight Players. But it gave her no great satisfaction. Soon enough he would be back with the Shakespeare Trust, and then Marianne would have him all to herself. A clear run to becoming the next Mrs Llewellyn. If anyone could do it *she* could. Already it appeared he was taking her down to Anglesey with him, and Carenza wondered agonisedly if they had become lovers. She thought it highly probable. Marianne wanted Gareth, and she wouldn't hesitate to use her considerable charms to weave herself into the fabric of his life. On and off stage, she would make herself part of him.

Carenza closed her eyes and her mind to the images conjured up, of Gareth with Marianne. Nevertheless, they sprang readily into being again when she arrived at rehearsal a little early, to find him already pacing the empty hall, and such a burning, all-consuming jealousy and sadness gripped her that she began to doubt her own sanity. It couldn't hurt that much! Oh, but it did!

'I'm glad you're here early,' he said. 'There's something I want to say to you that I prefer not to discuss in front of everyone else.'

Her heart began to thump unaccountably. 'I can't imagine we've anything that private to talk about,' she said with a contrived, icy dignity.

He shrugged this away impatiently. 'Oh, cut it out, Carenza. I know you're annoyed with me because I gave you a bit of advice you didn't relish, but that's trivial,' he said dismissively. 'I want to talk about you—your future.'

'My...future?' She stared at him doubtfully. For one crazy moment she entertained a wild, delicious fantasy that he was about to tell her he loved her. Then he said practically,

'Yes, your future. Your prospects. Watching you over these last weeks, I realise I wasn't mistaken about your potential. You could make it as an actress, Carenza, if you gave it a chance. Don't you think you owe it to yourself at least to try.'

Excitement rippled along her veins at the mere thought, and then subsided, just as swiftly.

'Gareth, I can't go back to drama school now. I've got financial and personal commitments.'

'I'm not talking about drama school,' he said. 'Not all actors come up that way. I didn't. I went straight into rep, and learned by doing. You're good enough for a company to take you on. Why don't you consider auditioning? I could give you some useful introductions.'

Her nervous, racing pulse skipped a few more beats. Dared she? Oh, it was too much, to have this dream dangled in front of her, years after she had given it up! And what if she did audition, and they turned her down—if she proved to be not good enough, and failed to justify his belief in her? Then she would have lost everything, even the little she had now—the thought that she *might* have made it, if only she'd had the chance.

'Oh...I don't know...' she said dubiously.

To her complete amazement, he seemed to galvanise suddenly; seizing her by the shoulders, he shook her roughly, angrily.

'Carenza! Come out from that hole and stop acting like a scared rabbit!' he exclaimed furiously. 'Start living, damn it! Start using everything you've got, instead of only fifty per cent!'

Her startled eyes looked into his, wide and revealing, and as her gaze locked with his, and his fingers dug into her shoulders, a fierce, dangerous and erratic current began to oscillate between them, awakening a thousand dormant connections. She heard his breath become ragged, saw desire leap in his eyes, and felt her own frenzied response to it in every part of her body. If he didn't take her in his arms this very minute and make love to her she thought she would die, and, at this very minute, the look on his face was telling her he felt the same.

Voices outside the hall brought her back to herself, unwillingly and with great difficulty. The others were arriving. Gareth turned his back on her, and she fought to convince herself that she had indeed seen that expression in his eyes, and not imagined it. In that moment, he had wanted her, she was sure, just as he had that afternoon at Plas Gwyn, when she had refused him.

Nothing had changed. He still did not love her. Probably the only woman he loved, still, was Celia, in spite of how she had wronged him. Possibly he was involved in an affair with Marianne, and it was certain he would soon be going out of Carenza's life for good. But she knew that if they had been certain, then, of an hour alone, without interruption, and he had started making love to her, she would gladly have met him halfway.

This tremendous insight into her own depths should have cast her down, but, contrarily, it filled Carenza with a strange, unholy elation. She was a woman. She loved—she functioned. Blazing with mystical power, she went on stage and gave Gareth a Desdemona he would not forget, shining with a pure and innocent sensuality that was breathtaking.

Perhaps this new, incandescent Carenza was simply too much for Nigel to match. He did his best, but the final act, where Othello, consumed by jealousy, strangled his entirely guiltless young wife in their bedchamber, failed to achieve the immense and tragic pathos needed to convince the audience of its awful inevitability.

'Nigel,' Gareth said quietly. 'You love her. You've killed her. And now you've realised that you were wrong, that all your suspicions were just fantasies Iago craftily induced you to believe. Can you go on living with this knowledge?'

There was only one way to get the message across. Mere explanations would not suffice. Gareth smiled wryly, and took the stage.

'Right,' he said softly. 'Let's take it again from "O, banish me, my lord, but kill me not." Carenza?'

He had his hands around her throat before she realised he was going to play Othello himself. As any director would, he had demonstrated with odd lines, speeches, snippets, but never the biggest part of a scene, playing opposite her. And now here she was, on stage with Gareth Llewellyn, as Celia so often must have been, playing the part of the wife he believed to be unfaithful. She couldn't do it— all her nerves were paralysed. She *had* to do it. It had been inevitable since that stormy day on a Welsh beach.

'*Carenza,*' he prompted her again, more urgently.

Then her other self took over, and she was no longer Carenza. A stronger magic than she had ever known worked its spell—she became Desdemona, and Gareth *was* Othello. The emotions the master of dramatists had written so skilfully came to life in both of them, and, although it was only a rehearsal in a church hall, no one who took part, or watched, could doubt that this was a performance of the finest quality.

Gareth spoke Othello's final speech with Carenza's inert body in his arms, and in the moment when he stabbed himself, taking his own life and falling across her, his lips against hers, a long shudder of horror ran through the room. And then there was a deep silence.

Releasing her gently, he grinned cheerfully around the stunned and still silent assembly.

'That's all for tonight, I think,' he said unconcernedly, as if it were nothing unusual.

It was Nigel who broke the spellbound hush. 'I'll never do it like that,' he said morosely.

Gareth clapped him on the shoulder and grinned again. 'But you'll do it,' he said. And, digging his hands into his jacket pockets, he strolled out, whistling tunelessly.

Only Carenza heard the echo of his voice—"I'm through with all that . . . I can never act on stage again." Well, tonight he had. Not in public, it was true, but he had acted. Had he simply been unable to resist showing them how it should be done, or had he broken that vow deliberately to demonstrate to her, Carenza, what *she* was capable of? What she was intent on denying herself?

She lingered behind that night, after the others left, feeling unable, as yet, to face the busy streets full of people and traffic. She wanted to savour briefly and alone the memory of herself on stage with Gareth. To come to terms with the experience.

'Coming?' Nigel asked.

She shook her head, smiling. 'No. You go. I'll lock up the hall.'

'Sure you couldn't use some company?'

'Not right now. Thanks all the same.' She was firm but gentle. If he truly did care for her, she sympathised. She knew only too well how it felt to love someone who could not love you in return.

Alone, she wandered into the room they used as a female dressing-room. It wasn't luxury—a row of pegs for hanging clothes, a sink with a mirror and a strip light over it, a battered old couch that had seen better days. The stuff that dreams were made on? She had reached out and touched her own dreams, tonight. Dared she do more?

She heard his footfall then, and long before she turned around to see him watching her from the doorway she knew it was him. It was going dark, the room was full of shadows, but he was real, and here; she felt herself vibrate with the nearness of him.

'Why did you come back?' she asked simply.

'Why are you still here?' he replied quietly. 'The answer is the same, Carenza.'

She did not move as he came towards her, stopping only when he was so close that she could feel the natural male warmth of him. The old Carenza would have flinched, stepped back, pushed him away. This new, as yet unrecognisable self stood still, trembling only slightly, and that with anticipation as he took her face between his hands, bent his head and kissed her. Long, slow and explorative, that kiss, drawing out a deep shudder of sensation from her very roots, but it was only a prelude, she knew.

Unhurriedly, and with great sensuality, he began to undress her, dealing with buttons and hooks with hands that never faltered or fumbled. He did not require her help, and she did not offer it—this slow unveiling was part of his lovemaking, and she submitted to it in a willing trance. Only when he lifted her, as easily as he had done on stage, and laid her on the couch, did his hands begin to discover her, gently at first, then more urgently, his lips following their progress until she cried out in desire, wanting him to fulfil this fierce need in her without delay.

He would not give her that swift, immediate satisfaction, and, without realising at first what she was doing, she found her fingers unbuttoning his shirt, running over his chest and shoulders, drawing him to her in a fever of impatience. Stretching his naked length against her, he whispered teasingly, 'No, Carenza, my impatient little one, not yet,' and continued to drive her wild with kisses and caresses until she thought she could endure it no longer.

When at last he entered her, she was as ready as he, and, although she was new and untouched, there was only the merest hint of pain before her rhythm matched his, and they moved together, as one. Carenza felt she was climbing a ladder to heaven, rung by rung, each powerful but gentle thrust taking her higher, until she reached the exquisite topmost stair, and ladder and all fell away beneath her, no longer needed. She was him, and he was her. All her loneliness, all her fears were gone, and she floated free in a new world of love and perfect confidence.

For a while they simply lay in each other's arms, fulfilled and speechless. And then Carenza turned her head against his shoulder, her dark mass of hair tumbling across his chest, and drifted off into the most serene sleep her life had ever known. It seemed forever, but might have been only minutes, for when her eyes blinked open she found herself covered by one of the old rugs that were always on the couch, and there were sounds she dazedly identified as the kettle boiling, mugs clattering.

She pulled herself up on one elbow, and saw Gareth, in his black cords, but still naked to the waist, making coffee. He smiled a little wry smile as he saw she was awake, and brought the coffee over, perching on the couch beside her.

Carenza took the mug in one hand, and pulled the rug up to cover herself better with the other. Suddenly she felt ridiculously shy, even though she recognised her action as pointless after all the things they had so recently been doing to one another.

'Gareth, I——'

He touched her lips briefly with his fingers.

'Sh. No need to say anything,' he told her gravely. 'No excuses, no explanations. It was what we both wanted, have wanted, of each other for some time. And it was beautiful in itself.'

He paused, looking at her with thoughtful tenderness.

'I know it was the first time for you,' he said. 'For me—well, it felt like that, too, after so long. Thank you for making me a man again.'

She stared at him, confused, and without thinking said the first thing that came into her head. 'After so long...? But...what about Marianne?'

He frowned. 'What about Marianne? Had you somehow got the idea that she and I were lovers?'

'I know she was with you on Anglesey, the other weekend,' Carenza stammered, nonplussed. 'I naturally concluded...'

The frown deepened. 'Then you shouldn't conclude. Haven't you listened to anything I've said to you, about my feelings with regard to women, over the last few months?' A hard edge had invaded the tenderness of his voice, and she shivered, drawing the rug closer about her. 'Yes, Marianne was there. She came down uninvited, and went back the same day. I know what she's up to, and the position she's seeking isn't on offer.'

Something cold and unpleasant seeped its way into Carenza's newly found joy.

'Are you trying to tell me that this... tonight...was no more than casual sex?' she ventured carefully. 'That you took me...but you don't care about me?'

'I care about you,' he said quietly. 'I want to see you go forward, forge ahead, realise your potential, both as an actress and as a human being. This was about release, Carenza—for both of us. You need never again be afraid of feelings you experienced tonight.'

She sat up, horrified, setting the cup down heavily on the floor, the rug falling away, leaving her naked and vulnerable, her face contorted with despair. How could he ever think that she would feel like that with another man? As if he had directed her in a new role, and, henceforth, all she needed to do was press a button and all those emotions, all those sensations, would come rushing back, on tap?

'But...but Gareth...I *love* you,' she whispered painfully.

He shook his head sagely, his eyes softer now, but there was an awful implacability about him as he said firmly, 'No, you don't. You only think you do, because I'm the first man who made love to you,' he said. 'I'm not Othello, and you aren't Desdemona. Your life is really only just beginning, and you have far—so far to go, Carenza. Mine is in the twilight, emotionally speaking. I'll work again, possibly I'll act, and maybe I'll be involved occasionally with women. But love isn't on my agenda. You knew that all along.'

A desperate, shameful anger was her saviour. Scrambling off the couch, she began to pull on her clothes, quickly, untidily, not caring how she looked.

'You're right!' she cried bitterly. 'It was no more than a spill-over of the parts we were playing on stage. I don't love you! When I do fall in love, I'll choose a man who's whole and capable of loving *me*, not one who's hiding behind the memory of a woman who cheated on him!'

He leapt up, eyes ablaze with an angry passion fiercer than she had ever seen in him, and his strong hands closed around her throat, just as they had in rehearsal. But this time it was for real, and for a brief, terrifying moment she thought she had pushed him too far, and he truly was going to kill her.

Then he released his grip, turned his back on her and shrugged into his shirt, buttoning it up and tucking it into his trousers before he faced her again. His expression now was cold and tightly controlled.

'If you have any sense at all of what's good for you, then I'd advise you to leave it at that, and say nothing more,' he warned her icily.

'That's fine by me. I have nothing more to say,' she replied, matching his cold demeanour with her own frozen dignity. And, picking up her bag, her script and her books, she preceded him out of the hall in silence.

# CHAPTER NINE

SOMEHOW, Carenza had expected that there would be a message from Gareth presenting his excuses and regretting that he could no longer continue directing the Spotlight Players. Perhaps he was too busy overseeing the furbishing of his new flat, or had decided to return to the Shakespeare Trust earlier than he had originally planned.

She could not have said which predominated: her fear of this happening—which meant that she would not see him again—or her fervent wish that it would, thus sparing her from facing him. How could she endure being in the same room with him, or being directed by him on stage, remembering how passionately she had responded to his loving— indeed, how she had welcomed and invited it, only to be summarily dismissed afterwards? As if it had merely been some medicine he had administered to her for her own good.

But she had reckoned without the sheer professionalism of the man. Gareth was there promptly on the next rehearsal night, crisp and businesslike, yet damnably relaxed. He treated Carenza no differently from the rest of the cast, and there was nothing in his manner, not even a brief look in his eye, or a softening of his voice, to betray that passionate hour spent in each other's arms. It might never have happened.

'Is there some problem, Carenza?' he demanded coolly, in an odd moment when no one was listening to them.

'No problem,' she retorted quickly. 'At least, not so far as I'm concerned. I didn't think you would come, that's all.'

'You think I'd let everyone down, at this stage in the proceedings?' His incredulity was tinged with scornful resentment. 'Whatever you may think of me personally, credit me with a little more dedication. I've never left a production halfway through. Even when——'

Even when Celia died, she knew he had been about to say, when someone interrupted them with a query. But she admitted to herself readily that she had been wrong in her estimate of his reactions. To Gareth Llewellyn, a production was a production; no matter if it were the Shakespeare Trust in their splendid purpose-built theatre in Birmingham or the Spotlight Players in a dusty church hall in Longbridge. It made no difference. Once committed, he would see it through.

And, it had to be said, there was a great sense of purposefulness and confidence about the amateur group right now, after all those weeks of intensive and inspired direction. Morale was sky high, and every member of the cast and of the backstage production team was fired up and ready to go. Scenery was being painted, props prepared, and they were awash with almost finished costumes. Posters had already been printed and circulated locally, and now, with opening night less than a week away, a fine, entirely natural and wholly necessary nervous tension had begun to tighten its grip on all of them.

Carenza felt it, probably more intensely than anyone else. She was like a complex engine, tuned up and running, ready and eager to do what she had been trained, coaxed and led towards throughout this unforgettable summer.

And if she still could not drive out of her heart her love for Gareth, if her treacherous body still ached for his touch, if his very presence was still the essential centre of her life—if that was so, well, there was nothing she could do to alter it. She had to live with it, accept it, and do her damnedest not to let him see how badly that need was eating away at her. She had to bury it deep inside her, and let her turbulent emotions find their only release on stage.

Wednesday was the first night of three consecutive performances, and on Tuesday afternoon Sammy arrived home. Bronwen, knowing how busy Carenza would be, had offered to bring the girl home by train. It was a long time since the hardworking farmer's wife had had a day or two away, she said, so she would come with Sammy to see the play, and perhaps do a little shopping, before returning to Anglesey on Thursday. Unfortunately, Dai was unable to accompany her. They couldn't both leave the farm at once, Carenza realised, but it was no great surprise to her when she saw that Trefor had come with them.

'It's going to be hard for the youngsters, being apart after spending practically the entire summer together,' Bronwen sympathised. 'I shall miss Sammy, too; I've loved having her around. She's been like another daughter, and so helpful around the farm.'

Carenza watched her young sister and Trefor together with a deep, careful interest. They were very young, true enough, but the big-brother attitude he had always adopted with her in the past, teasing and casually proprietorial, had been replaced by a new protectiveness. However, there was nothing awkward about the relationship. They were at ease and comfortable together.

'We wondered,' Sammy said hesitantly, 'that is, Bronwen says it's OK, if you don't mind...could I go back to Anglesey with her and Trefor on Thursday? It's the last chance before school starts next Tuesday, and, after all, you're going to be busy with the play for the next few days.'

Carenza saw how important it was to her, and she didn't have the heart to refuse.

'All right,' she said. 'Why not? I can drive down myself on Saturday and spend the weekend, then we can come back together on Monday. When the play's over, I shall be ready for a rest.'

And it will give me something to do, other than think about Gareth, she added to herself. Gareth, whose role in her life would then be over, who would have gone back to his real existence and his work with the Shakespeare Trust. Also to Marianne St John, who, although he had said he was not involved with her, had only to be there, biding her time, until the right moment arrived. *She* would be too clever to show her hand and embarrass him by spilling out unwanted protestations of love, Carenza was sure!

At dress rehearsal on Tuesday, everything that could possibly go wrong did so. Lines were fluffed, costumes tripped over, and the follow spot turned temperamental, and had to be coaxed to work at all. Everyone was fraught, tempers were frayed, and Carenza, like the rest of the cast, was convinced that the performance was going to be a monumental disaster.

'Don't worry about it,' Gareth said calmly, as they all sat drinking coffee afterwards in a state of nervous exhaustion. 'Don't you know that a bad dress rehearsal signifies a good first night? That's an old theatrical tradition.'

They all stared doubtfully at him, and he raised his mug in a cheerful toast.

'To you—Spotlight Players. It really *will* be all right on the night,' he promised them. 'I have faith in you—and I know it.'

Wednesday was a mad rush of last-minute costume alterations, skimped, unwanted meals, and shattered nerves, and by the time she arrived at the church hall Carenza's heart was going at a steady knock, and she felt as if she were preparing for her own public execution.

Peering out through the curtains at the rows of seats, just beginning to fill up, she knew a moment of sheer, blind, unreasoning panic. Why do I do this? she asked herself woodenly. Because I'm crazy? Because I have this deep, irrational need to make an utter idiot of myself in public? Because it's compulsive, like nail-biting, and I can't help it, she answered herself ruefully, escaping the waiting nemesis of the audience for the chaos of the dressing-room.

Gareth had assured them that, although no one was to know of the part he had played in rescuing their production, he would be there, on first night, to the bitter end. And indeed he had been much in evidence throughout the day; his help, his encouragement, and the sheer buoyant enthusiastic drive of his personality had kept them all going. But Carenza had seen little or nothing of him alone, and their personal relationship was now nonexistent, she thought sadly. Defunct. Well and truly over.

Now, hurrying to the dressing-room, she all but ran full tilt into a familiar figure.

'Perry!' she exclaimed, astonished. 'When did you get back?'

'Yesterday.' Their old director looked quiet, chastened, but in control of himself. 'I went to stay with my parents, and then spent most of the summer at their holiday cottage in Devon. I was pretty shattered at first, but after a while I started to feel bad about leaving you all in the lurch. I came back to apologise, and found you had acquired the services of someone far better qualified than I am!'

'Everyone understood your reasons,' Carenza assured him quickly. 'And Gareth only stepped in temporarily, to help us out of a spot. No one is supposed to know about it.'

'So he told me. We had a long talk, earlier,' Perry said. 'I have to say how splendid I think it is that someone so famous, so...so celebrated was prepared to do so much for an amateur society. And full marks to you for persuading him, Carenza.'

'But I didn't,' she said. 'It was all his own idea.'

He looked puzzled. 'Oh? That's strange,' he said. 'From what he told me, I somehow got the idea that he had done it all for you.'

Carenza gave a wry laugh. 'You must have misunderstood him. Maybe he felt impelled to help me because he thinks I once did him a good turn, but you shouldn't read too much into that,' she said. 'Gareth has his own inscrutable reasons for everything he does, and they're not always the ones he gives.'

She hesitated. 'But what about you—will you be back at school on Tuesday?'

'Do I have a choice? I still have to pay the mortgage on the house my wife and children are living in,' he said ruefully.

Carenza gave his hand a sympathetic squeeze.

'And...Lynne? How are things there?' she asked cautiously.

'I'm going to see the kids at the weekend. We've agreed to talk,' he said. 'Where it will lead from there, I don't know, but it's a beginning. We'll see.'

He glanced at his watch. 'Go on now, Carenza. You've still got your make-up to do. Everyone's been telling me about your fantastic Desdemona, and I'm agog to see it.'

The flutter of nerves she had suppressed while talking to Perry returned in full force as she got ready, tense and tight-lipped, more nervous than ever before, because if she did not come across tonight for the rest of her life she would feel she had let Gareth down. And however badly their personal affairs had ended she could not deny all he had done for the Spotlight Players, and for her own individual progress as an actress. Oh, lord, just let me be good tonight, she prayed, and I'll never ask for anything else!

She was putting the finishing touches to her make-up when Teresa, the prompter, put her head round the door.

'Special delivery!' she grinned. 'Flowers for the leading lady! I'd say you have a secret but very classy admirer, Carenza!'

Exclamations of pleasure and envy ran round the room as Carenza brought in the huge basket with its arrangement of white, pink and red roses, carnations, ferns, and lilies of the valley. The flowers were so fresh that their petals were still damp, and their fragrance filled the air, competing with the odours of greasepaint and perspiration.

Carenza buried her face in them briefly, and in a moment all her fears subsided. Power and confidence began to flow back into her. The small card in the centre of the arrangement carried a message of only one brief line, unsigned, but that did not matter. To wish anyone 'good luck' just before going on stage was to invite the opposite, and this, then, was his final gift to her.

"Break a leg, Carenza", Gareth Llewellyn had written. And, setting the flowers on the dressing-table with a small smile, she left the dressing-room and took her place in the wings.

'I knew you were good, of course, because I've seen you act before,' Sammy confided next morning, perched on the end of her sister's bed. 'But I never knew you were *that* good. Like a *real* actress!'

Carenza smiled as she sipped the tea Sammy had made—as usual, it was far too strong, and thick with sugar.

'Everyone was good,' she said, with quiet satisfaction. 'Nothing went wrong—at least, nothing that anyone out front could notice! If the next two nights follow suit, I shan't complain!'

'Yes, I think even good old Nigel didn't do too badly at all, as Othello, although I reckon you carried him, sis,' Sammy said proudly. 'You really were fantastic. I just hope some of the kids at school see you, then I can bask in your reflected glory for a full term!'

'Get along with you!' Carenza laughed, but she could not hide her pleasure.

It was true—*Othello* had been a resounding success. She would not have believed it, only a few weeks ago, when they had been on the point of giving it up.

'We have Gareth to thank for most of it,' she admitted soberly. 'He hauled us up by our bootstraps and hammered us into shape. I don't suppose he particularly needs the kudos, but it seems a shame we couldn't acknowledge his help.'

He had been there, backstage, all night, watchful and encouraging, his mere presence a support in itself. Carenza had caught his eyes on her, once, as she waited for her entrance, and she had wanted to say, Thank you for the flowers, and for everything else you gave me that was good—no matter how it ended.

But he had merely given her a little, warning shake of the head, as if to say, No more. Leave it at that, and she had accepted that the time was not right. After the performance, she would find a moment to thank him gracefully.

Applause as the final curtain fell had been thunderously appreciative, and they took repeated calls, all smiling and bowing, glowing with the pleasure of achievement. Then someone in the audience had called out, 'Director!' and the call was taken up. Carenza glanced towards the wings, where Gareth stood, hidden from view, and she saw him smile and gently propel Perry on to the stage.

'I feel a fraud!' he whispered between gritted teeth, as he bowed with the rest of them. 'I never intended to steal his praise!'

Carenza understood perfectly what Gareth had done. The Spotlight Players had been Perry's baby for a long time. This summer, under intolerable stress, he had briefly deserted them, but he would want to come back. And, since Gareth's own involvement had to be a secret, this was his way of handing Perry back his place.

'It's the way he wants it, Perry,' she said quietly. 'Smile—and welcome back.'

After the curtain had fallen for the last time, and the audience had left, there was the usual first-night backstage party for the cast, their families and friends, with sandwiches, vol-au-vents, chicken drumsticks and fancy cakes provided by the long-suffering partners of the Spotlight Players. There was champagne, too, and as the corks began to pop Carenza looked round in vain for the one person with whom she needed to share her triumph. But there was no sign of him.

'Where's Gareth?' she asked, trying to sound supremely casual. 'I saw him just before the final curtain call.'

'He left, five minutes ago,' Teresa told her. 'I tried to persuade him to stay—after all, we couldn't have done it without him, but he said he had to go. He left a whole crate of champagne—and I think there's a note on the box.'

Carenza picked up the envelope and opened it with tremulous fingers. Everyone fell suddenly quiet, and she took a firm grip on herself as she realised she was expected to read it out.

"It's all yours from now on, Spotlight Players," she read quietly, and, sure enough, the handwriting was the same as that on the card inside her flowers. "Congratulations. Perhaps you needed me no more than I needed you. Yours in spirit—Gareth."

Cryptic to the last, she thought, sipping her champagne and trying to keep the smile fixed on her face. It had been a wonderful night. She was supposed to be happy. Only she knew that her love had gone, and that her heart had gone with him. Only she knew that she could never feel this way about anyone else, ever again. Keep smiling, Carenza. Maybe some day the hurt will fade, and you'll be able to face the rest of your life without him. Only keep smiling.

Thursday's performance, although it did not have the same excitement generated by the first night, went equally well. Gareth would have been proud of them, Carenza thought sadly, fighting back a tear. She was glad that Perry was there, doing whatever he could to help and encourage, but was surprised when he sought her out afterwards, wearing a rather odd expression on his face.

'There's a man wants to see you,' he said. 'I've put him in the little room at the back, where the vicar does his paperwork.'

She sighed. 'A man? What does he want? I'm awfully tired, and I was just about to go home,' she said wearily.

'I think it would be in your interests to see him, Carenza,' Perry urged. 'He showed me his card—he's a theatrical agent.'

If he had expected her to react with excitement he was disappointed, and Carenza herself could not understand why her heart failed to give a nervous leap at the words. Perhaps all her emotions had been drained on stage. Or perhaps she had expended them all on Gareth, and now that he was gone she quite simply had nothing left.

'Oh, all right, I suppose I had better see him,' she said listlessly.

Joseph Bergland was not remotely what Carenza had expected a theatrical agent to look like. He wasn't big and flamboyant, didn't smoke a king-sized cigar, or wear a coat with a fur collar. In fact, he was a mousy little man with a sharp nose and horn-rimmed glasses. But his eyes were shrewd and all-seeing, his manner knowledgeable.

'I don't usually go hunting for talent in amateur productions,' he said, proffering her his card. 'To be honest, one rarely finds anything better than—well, amateurs. But someone left me a cutting from the local paper, with a write-up of last night's performance, and a little note saying that it might be worth my while.'

Gareth, Carenza thought wryly. Still guiding her from the wings, still trying to push her in the direction he thought she should take. She did not know whether to feel flattered that he thought she merited his efforts, or resentful of his interference. Surely he wasn't simply trying to make amends for his rejection of her? He wouldn't waste this man's time and professional expertise if he didn't think she was good enough?

No, because, even before they had made love, he had tried to convince her she should audition, Carenza remembered. The prospect had set her pulse racing then. Wasn't it what she had always wanted? So why could she raise not a flicker of enthusiasm now?

'I think you've got rare promise, Miss Carlton,' Joseph Bergland said seriously. 'You're inexperienced, sure, and you have a lot to learn, but it's all there, ready to come to life under the right conditions. I'd like to have you on my books, and I'm fairly sure I could launch you on a theatrical career.'

Carenza smiled warily. 'That's very gratifying, Mr Bergland, and it's good of you to take time out to come and see me,' she said politely.

'It's not good of me at all—it's my business, and I expect to profit from it,' he said practically. 'You're a real find. Whoever sent me that cutting did us both a service.'

'But Mr Bergland,' Carenza sighed, 'I'm not at all sure that he did.'

The agent appeared flabbergasted. 'Let me get this straight. Are you telling me that you don't want to go on the professional stage?'

'I'm telling you that I don't think it's possible,' she said. 'I'm a teacher, with a mortgage to pay and a sister to support. Even if you could guarantee me work, I couldn't leave her alone and go gallivanting around the country.'

Joseph Bergland frowned. He seemed puzzled by the whole business of this girl's failure to leap at his offer with open arms, where he usually had to fend off prospective hopefuls wanting passionately to tread the boards.

'Don't turn this down out of hand,' he begged. 'Think about it. I'll leave you my card, and you can give me a ring when you've had time to consider. Then we can talk terms. You could always find a good boarding-school for your sister.'

Send Sammy to boarding-school? Never, Carenza vowed. She would hate it. She only tolerated Longbridge Comprehensive because she knew she could escape from it at the end of every day!

But she promised the agent that she would give his offer some thought—more to get rid of him than because she seriously thought it was possible for her to accept.

Back home in the flat, quiet and empty now Sammy had gone back to Anglesey with Bronwen and Trefor, she made herself a cup of coffee, kicked off her shoes, and sank wearily into a chair.

A few months ago, she reflected, she would have been wild with joy if anyone had even suggested she was capable of acting professionally, let alone offered to take her under his wing. Now here was this man wanting to put her on his books, and at the recommendation of no less a personage than Gareth Llewellyn.

She should have been over the moon! Even if she had regretfully been obliged to turn him down because of Sammy, she should have been aching with disappointment. Were all her long-buried ambitions truly dead, after all? It was ironic that it was Gareth who had brought her fully to life as an actress, and Gareth who, conversely, appeared to have killed the spark that motivated her.

You're stupid, she told herself. You've lost him. Well, to be honest, you never really had him, only briefly. You never had his love. Are you going to waste the rest of your life bemoaning what you knew all along could not be yours?

By Friday, everyone in the Spotlight Players had heard that Carenza had been approached by a theatrical agent, and most of them agreed she was mad not to jump at the opportunity being held out to her.

'Let's face it, you're the only one among us who has that sort of talent,' Briony said briskly. 'You owe it to yourself at least to give it a shot. If it doesn't work, you could always go back to teaching, but Carenza, I'm sure you could make it. Please try!'

'Carenza has responsibilities, remember,' Nigel said primly. 'She knows she can't just walk out on them.'

'No one is suggesting that she does any such thing,' Francis put in quietly. 'But Carenza—just think how your sister would feel if you gave up this opportunity on her account. She would always blame herself, and feel she had held you back. She'd hate that—and you wouldn't want her carrying such a load of guilt.'

Carenza jumped abruptly to her feet. 'Well, thank you all for sorting out my life for me!' she exclaimed crossly. Then, calming down a little, she regretted her angry words. 'I'm sorry—I know you have my interests at heart. But it's not a decision I can take hastily, and without a lot of thought.'

'We understand,' Francis said gently. 'Perhaps, once the play's over, you can take some time.'

She cast him a grateful look. 'How you manage to be such a mean old Iago on stage, I shall never know,' she laughed.

She could not tell any of them, of course, that it wasn't only her worries about Sammy that were causing her to hold back. How much any of them had guessed or suspected of her feelings for Gareth she had no way of knowing, but none of them knew just how far things had gone between them, and how much she was now suffering on account of it.

All at once, quite suddenly, she was overwhelmed by a longing for Anglesey. The calm green fields and the sharp tang of the sea. The towering stack of Holyhead, and the misty mountains of the Lleyn Peninsula, away in the distance. The peace and solitude, the unhurried certainties of an older, less frenetic way of life, that were the boundaries of Dai's and Bronwen's little world.

There she would go to think, to work out the direction her life must take—as she had done once before, many years ago. And there, perhaps, some of the pain would . . . well, not fade, for she was sure that in a sense it would always be with her . . . but she could find a way to bear it. She would come back, if not whole, at least patched together so that the cracks did not show.

And now she was sure Gareth would not be there. He had returned to Birmingham, to the Shakespeare Trust and the worldwide acclaim he had, for a while, eschewed, but which would soon be his again. She could walk on the beach and remember him. How they had met, and how he had over-turned her life. She could gaze at Plas Gwyn, empty once more, from a distance, and hear again in her imagination his beautiful voice, harsh with scorn, or tender with desire. She could commit it all to memory, once and for all. And then she would try to forget.

In a calmer, steadier frame of mind, Carenza put on her costume and her make-up, and went out on stage where, for the final time, she loved, suffered and died as Desdemona.

# CHAPTER TEN

CARENZA'S sister was waiting for her as she drove up to the caravan on Saturday, and, instead of swinging on the gate she opened it decorously for Carenza to drive through, then closed it carefully behind her.

She was wearing a *skirt*, Carenza noted incredulously, for the only skirt Sammy usually wore was her school uniform, and she complained mightily about that. But here she was, in a skirt and a sweater Carenza had not seen before, and shoes with neat little heels.

'Like the outfit?' she asked cheerily, observing her sister's stunned regard. 'I bought it in Holyhead with the money you gave me. Well, you said it was time I had something decent to wear.'

Carenza looked disbelievingly from Sammy to Trefor at her side then back again. 'I keep saying that, but you generally just go out and buy more jeans.'

'I've got enough jeans,' her sister said loftily. 'Lunch is ready. It's cold, of course, because I didn't know what time you'd be here. See you later, then, Trefor.'

'OK, Samantha.'

Carenza watched him lope across the field to the farmhouse. She had the oddest sensation of having inadvertently wandered on to the wrong set.

*'Samantha?'*

The girl shrugged, a little sheepishly. 'Oh, well ... Sammy was all right when I was little, but it sounds a bit babyish now,' she said. 'You don't mind, do you?'

'Me?' Carenza was about to point out that it was Sammy herself who had always insisted on the abbreviation, then she bit her tongue diplomatically. 'Of course not. It'll take me a little time to get used to it, though, so you'll have to bear with me if I forget now and then.'

Bemused, she followed her sister into the caravan. Sammy had made a very passable quiche, prepared salad to accompany it, and there was a chocolate cake for afterwards.

'I must say, this is very good,' Carenza said, accepting a second piece.

'It's Bronwen's recipe, but I made it myself. I like cooking,' her sister stated. 'You can see the point to it. Who knows? One day I might even be as good a cook as you.' She cut herself yet another huge slice, reassuring Carenza that, whatever else had changed, her appetite was unimpaired. 'Oh, by the way, we're going to the cinema this afternoon, Trefor and me. That's if you don't——'

'Trefor and I,' Carenza corrected automatically. 'And no, I don't mind. I've got to unpack and have a shower. I still feel as if I'm encrusted with several layers of stage make-up.'

'Right,' Sammy laughed. 'You can have the place all to yourself for the afternoon. But tonight we're having dinner with Dai and Bronwen.'

So much for my solitary weekend of long, thoughtful walks and self-examination, Carenza thought, grinning ruefully. It would just have to wait until tomorrow.

That night, she and Sammy curled up at opposite ends of the window-seat in the caravan, drinking their late-night cocoa and gazing out at the lights of Holyhead, twinkling bravely but upstaged by a vast, dark night sky, ablaze with stars.

Dinner had been the usual uproarious occasion, with lots of talk and laughter, and several weeks in their midst had virtually turned Samantha into one of the Pritchards. Carenza, while she was thankful for the way her sister had been accepted as a full member of the household, could not help but feel herself at a slight distance.

'You certainly appear to have settled down here well,' she remarked.

'No problem,' Sammy said emphatically. 'Everyone has been wonderful, and treated me just like one of the family. But you know I've always loved it here, and now——'

She checked herself, and Carenza smiled gently.

'Now it's you and Trefor, you're even happier,' she said.

Her sister coloured. 'How did you know?'

Carenza chuckled. 'Love, it isn't hard to work out, although to be honest Bronwen spotted how you felt before I did. But take it easy. You're still very young.'

Sammy gave a knowing little grin. 'People get more sensible when they get older, do they?' she retorted. 'It didn't help you very much with Gorgeous Gareth, did it?'

Carenza looked up sharply, almost spilling her cocoa. 'What do you mean?'

'I know you're in love with him,' Sammy said calmly. 'Don't worry, I haven't said anything to anyone else, and you put on a fair show of hiding it. But why? If he knew, perhaps you would find out that he felt the same way.'

Carenza shook her head. 'I can promise you there's not a chance of that,' she said firmly. This was not territory she could share with a young sister, even one who was growing up as fast as Sammy. She had given Gareth her love. She had also given him her virginity. He had taken the one, and firmly rejected the other. 'People like Gareth are not for such as you and me,' she told her sister.

'People like Gareth have the same feelings you and I have,' Sammy persisted stubbornly. 'He's not a Martian.'

'I know, pet, but... he belongs to the professional theatre; he's acclaimed, famous... he moves in a very different world.'

'You could belong to that world,' her sister said, in a quiet, suddenly very mature voice. 'You *could*, Carenza. If you wanted.'

They stared at each other in silence for a while, and Carenza realised she could no longer treat this aware young person as a child, keeping everything difficult and potentially painful from her.

At length, she said, 'There's something I should tell you. A theatrical agent came to see me on Thursday night. He wants to put me on his books.'

Sammy gripped both her hands and squeezed them hard.

'That's great! Go for it, sis! You know it's what you've always wanted!' she urged. 'You gave it up once, for me—I know you did. So here's a second chance! Take it!'

'Sammy... Samantha... it's not that simple,' Carenza said slowly. 'It would mean giving up my teaching job. There's the flat... I would probably have to travel quite a lot . . . and think, you haven't finished school yet. When you do, you might want to go on to college, and . . .'

'You must be joking!' Samantha said with a snort. 'In case you've forgotten, I'm fifteen next week. I can leave school when I'm sixteen, and I'm not planning to stay on a day longer than I have to! You must know that A Levels and college and all that stuff aren't my style!'

'Maybe not. But your sixteenth birthday is still a year away,' Carenza objected. 'You still have to finish your education.'

'OK. But I could board here with Dai and Bronwen, leaving you free to get on with your career,' Sammy said. 'I know they'd have me. There's a perfectly good school in Holyhead, and I could bus in with Joanna. You could come down to stay whenever you got the chance, and you would know I'd be all right.'

'Steady on!' Carenza got up, and began pacing up and down the lounge area. 'You're moving too fast for me, young woman!'

Sammy giggled, then immediately sobered. 'Carenza, I know I'm only fourteen, but I'm quite sure that this is where I want to be, when I'm grown up. Here on the farm, with the animals, and the sea. And Trefor. I think, in a way, I've always known that, just as you knew, when you were my age, that you wanted to act. That was your thing. This is mine.'

Carenza stopped pacing. Her face was grave and serious as she regarded her young sister, troubled for a few moments. Then she smiled, as she experienced that lightening of the spirits that came

with recognising and acknowledging an essential
truth.

It wasn't for Sammy, the long, academic slog
through college, the life of a city career girl. What
was right for her was the open air life, the farm
with its steady, seasonal rhythms, a fairly young
marriage to a boy she had always known, who
would provide her with a steadfast, if quiet love
and security. Children, animals, sea and sky—
continuity.

'Yes,' she said finally. 'Perhaps you're right. Let's
sleep on it now. Give me a little space to sort myself
out, and then we'll plan accordingly.' She ventured
a grin at the girl who, overnight, it seemed, was no
longer a child but a junior partner. 'Does that suit
you?'

'You bet.' Sammy leaned over and gave her a
brief, affectionate hug before heading for her
bedroom.

Sunday morning on Anglesey. A slight mist, which
had drifted in from the sea and cloaked the shore
during the night, just rolling away, and the sun
breaking through, promising a fine, sunny day
without the fierce intensity of high summer. Sounds
of cattle and sheep, and the cry of a lone gull disturbing the silence, but only adding to the deep
sense of peace and changelessness.

A morning like so many others Carenza had spent
here over the years, and yet unlike. And since
everything else was the same it had to be herself
who had altered. Everything here now served to
remind her of Gareth, and probably always would,
whenever she came here in the future. She had not
escaped the pain of loving him—if anything, it was

intensified by her very surroundings. Had she forgotten how closely this place was bound up with her memories of him?

'I'm going for a long walk,' she said to Sammy after breakfast. 'I've got some thinking to do, and I need to be alone to do it.'

'No problem,' her sister said steadily. 'There are plenty of places hereabouts where you can be alone. Joanna and I are going for a swim—unless Bronwen finds some chores for us to do first, which she probably will.'

Carenza deliberately avoided walking in the direction of Plas Gwyn. She wasn't ready, yet, to face looking at Gareth's house and reliving the few but eventful hours she had spent there. Instead, she set off across the beach, up the headland and along the coastal path, keeping up a steady pace until she reached the point where she could look out across the wide expanse of Church Bay, with the sea shimmering unbroken all the way to Ireland.

Almost unconsciously she found herself scrambling down to the small cove where once she and Gareth had performed the love scene from *Othello*. How naïve and ignorant she had been then; how little she had known about the powerful currents of love that swirled beneath the calm surface of life, to surge up, suddenly, in a tidal wave of emotions. Emotions she had struggled to express in her acting, without ever having experienced them.

She perched uncomfortably on a rock and watched the sea eddying up the beach towards her in little runnels, lace-edged with foam. And as she sat there, losing all sense of the passing minutes, it seemed to her that she was not alone. She felt his presence near her, and all about her, as if they had

entered into a solemn pact together on that day,
months ago, and he was still waiting, demandingly,
not prepared to release her from it.

Very well, Gareth, my beloved tyrant, she said
to herself, I'll do it. She would try. If she didn't,
she would never know whether she was good
enough or not, and the uncertainty would haunt
her always.

Sammy would be happier here, in Anglesey, than
anywhere else, Carenza was sure of that. For
herself, she could keep the flat in Longbridge as a
base, and venture out into the unknown, precarious world that was beckoning to her. If she
could not have Gareth's love, she would have the
next best thing—the joy of proving to him, and to
herself, that his faith in her had not been mis-
placed. It would be a long, hard haul, most likely,
fraught with pitfalls. She did not deceive herself
that she had only to step on stage to achieve instant
recognition and success. But if she had the talent,
and was prepared to work determinedly, Carenza
began, from that moment, to believe that she could
do it, and that she had to give it her best shot.

'Yes!' she said aloud. 'Yes, yes!' and a fierce
surge of resolution shook her, so that she wound
her arms around her body, hugging herself hard to
contain it. Her love for Gareth Llewellyn and her
burning need to act were interwound too closely to
be disentangled. She would never be free of either,
and if that was the way it had to be—well, fighting
such a current was like ordering back the ever-
encroaching sea.

'Are you understudying for a mermaid?' a dry
voice asked close behind her. 'The tide is coming

in. If you sit here for much longer you'll have to swim for shore.'

Incredulity made Carenza lose her balance, and she slipped from the rock, her feet landing in the cold wavelets that lapped around it. His arms reached out to steady her, turning her round and setting her straight, and as his warm hands touched her, and she looked up into his grave, brilliant grey eyes, she knew that he was real, not a blissful illusion her longing thoughts had conjured up.

'Gareth!' she said stupidly, still in a daze of painful delight at the sight of him, the feel of him. 'I thought you would be in Birmingham. I never expected to find you here.'

'But I fully expected to find you here, when you were not at your flat, and one of your neighbours said you had gone away,' he replied.

'You were looking for me?' she frowned, puzzled. 'Why?'

He glanced down at the incoming sea, now foaming around their ankles.

'Let's move, Carenza, unless we want more than our feet to get wet,' he suggested, and, taking her hand, he led her out of the cove. They scrambled part way back up the path to the cliffs, and sank down in a grassy, sheltered hollow. The sun was warm and strong, and the boom of the waves far below was the only sound, themselves the only human presence on this quiet, deserted shore.

Carenza found her gaze drawn to him irresistibly, and she realised he was regarding her with a quiet but intent scrutiny. All at once, her own heartbeat was painful to her; she was deeply aware of him, of his nearness, of their total isolation from all but one another.

Although she was fully dressed, she felt oddly naked, as if she were still on the dressing-room couch, waiting for him to make love to her. She wanted him still, wanted him now, and the knowledge that if he were to touch her, she would give herself to him willingly, this minute, left her without defences.

'I wasn't happy about the way we parted,' he said quietly. 'You covered it very well, during those last days of rehearsal, and I was proud of your . . . professionalism, for lack of a better word. But I sensed you were angry with me—because of what happened in the dressing-room that night.'

She fought a strong urge to look down, forcing herself to meet his eyes directly and unflinchingly.

'I was, at first,' she admitted. 'But you were right—I couldn't stay a virgin forever. If it hadn't been you, it would have been someone else. It's no big deal.'

The words cost her dearly, because they were not the truth that was in her heart, but a carefully considered response, calculated to salvage her pride and ease his feelings of guilt, thus releasing them both. But his reaction was not what she expected—a relieved acceptance. Instead, something very much like anger glittered in his eyes, and the lines of his expressive mouth narrowed.

'No big deal,' he repeated softly, disbelievingly. 'Is that what you think? Let me tell *you* something, girl.'

He shifted his position, turning slightly in profile to her, and staring straight ahead, out to sea.

'I went out into the car park that night, and got into my car. I even started the engine. I wrestled with myself, damn it! I told myself that you were too innocent, too inexperienced, that I had no right to complicate your life further, even though I wanted you so much it hurt.

'But something pulled me back. I could feel you calling me...feel that you wanted me, just as strongly, and I could not resist that call, Carenza. It was too powerful, too insistent.'

She swallowed hard, remembering how she had stood alone in the darkening room, aching with her need for him.

'I *did* want you, Gareth,' she confessed quietly. 'You were not mistaken about that. And maybe, yes, it was right for us to make love when we did. But I *was* innocent, and I suppose I didn't understand, right then, that it could happen that way, briefly, between two people...without strings, without commitment...and still be very good.'

She paused and drew in a deep breath before continuing.

'I made you angry, too, I know—because of what I said about you and Celia. I was way out of order, and I'm sorry.'

He gave a soft, derisive laugh, but the scorn, she saw with some surprise, was directed not at her, but at himself.

'Oh, no, you were quite right,' he said candidly, and without rancour. 'It was no less than the truth, and it needed saying. Only you, my courageous and foolish Carenza, had the gall to leap in and say it, where everyone else had been carefully pussy-footing around.'

He faced her again now, and he was smiling, a little ruefully.

'How did you know? Someone told you, that day at Plas Gwyn, I suppose,' he said. 'It must be so, because no one knew the truth, outside the Shakespeare Trust—and they all closed ranks very loyally around me.'

Carenza bit her lip, not feeling able to betray her source, for all she did not care for the woman very much, but Gareth was not deceived.

'It was Marianne, I reckon,' he said with a wry grin. 'Only she would consider that a clever thing to do. It doesn't matter, Carenza,' he added calmly. 'I don't care now who knows.'

'She said...she said you knew about Celia's affair yourself, all along,' Carenza almost whispered, for all they were quite alone, not sure how to take his confident, self-possessed treatment of a subject that would once have sunk him deep in depression or sent him wild with anger.

'Well, of course I did,' he said flatly. 'On some deep, unconscious level I was aware for some time that my marriage was not the perfect idyll the media hyped it up to be. To begin with, I wanted children—so did Celia, when we first married, or, at least, so she pretended. But she did an about-face on that, and kept putting it off for years, saying that it would ruin her career. As if we couldn't have managed to be parents and actors, too. I'm not such a male chauvinist that I'd have expected her to retire completely and forever!'

He seemed to look back into the past, briefly, before giving his attention fully back to her.

'When we finally did have the twins, Celia seemed almost to resent them. She was struggling on stage, too. It all seemed to be falling apart, and it was so sad, because in the beginning it *was* just as I described it to you. She *was* bright and beautiful, and we *were* in love.'

'Marianne said something about Celia's success being tied to your coat-tails,' Carenza ventured carefully. 'She said Celia was only good when she was on stage with you.'

He gave this long and thoughtful consideration before saying finally, 'Yes, that might well have been so. Maybe I didn't help much—I was impatient, and expected the same perfection she had always given me. It was perhaps inevitable that she would turn to someone else, but by then the heart had gone out of it for me, too. If it hadn't been for the children——'

He broke off, and now, when he talked about the poor, lost babies who had never grown up, Carenza could sense real pain radiating out from the inner core of him.

'You don't have to say any more, if you don't want to,' she said quickly, reaching out and briefly touching his hand. He clasped it between his, and as the contact between them was remade a familiar tingle jumped eagerly along her veins.

'Yes, I do, and I do *want* to,' he responded very firmly. 'I want you to understand what I finally understand myself.'

He let go her hand.

'I can't concentrate while I'm touching you,' he said, and her heart leapt—at least he still found her desirable. She had that knowledge to hug close to her, if nothing else. But she folded her hands primly in her lap as she listened to him.

'She skipped off to America without my prior knowledge or agreement,' he said. 'I would not have consented to the twins' going, no matter what she did. But I was on stage, and the first I heard was a phone call from Los Angeles. She'd taken

Concorde to New York and then caught the first connecting flight.'

'Weren't you furious?' Carenza asked, realising the question was unnecessary, as soon as she had phrased it. She could well imagine.

'What do you think?' He gave a short, reminiscent laugh. 'But I was committed to three performances of *Macbeth* in Stratford, and I didn't feel I could let down the rest of the cast, to say nothing of the audiences, so I decided that afterwards I would fly straight over and bring my children back. I didn't reckon on having to use much persuasion, let alone force. She'd only taken them to spite me. So I waited. If only I hadn't—then they might not have been on the flight that crashed.'

He was quiet for a moment, and Carenza said, 'You couldn't have known. Surely you can't blame yourself?'

'In a way, I do, and always will,' he replied soberly. 'I know it's illogical, but there it is. But one can't change the past. Events overtook me, and Celia decided she was coming back.'

'She failed the screen test,' Carenza supplied.

'Marianne told you that, too?' He raised his eyebrows, but Carenza saw that the grey eyes beneath them were once again clear and direct. 'Celia phoned me in tears. It had all been a mistake. She loved me and always had, et cetera, et cetera. She wanted to come back; it would all be as it was when we first met. And so on.' His voice was level, unemotional, and there was no bitterness in it. 'I told her I'd consider it. We had, after all, two children to think about. But I knew then what I know now—what, in all the trauma and tragedy of what followed, I managed to hide from myself—that I no longer loved her.'

The words fell quietly into the silence all around them, and Gareth smiled, with faint irony. 'That made my guilt all the worse, don't you see?' he said. 'If I'd loved her, I was the victim of a tragedy. If I didn't, it seemed, in some perverse way, a punishment I had brought upon myself. I couldn't take that, so I retreated behind the myth. The myth took over my life. It had begun to look frayed around the edges when I met you, but you stormed in, regardless, and dealt it a death blow.'

Carenza shook her head. 'Oh, Gareth, I didn't know that was what I was doing!' she cried. 'Talk about "where angels fear to tread"!'

'I'm glad you did rush in,' he said. 'And you...perhaps you've gained just a little from your encounter with the mad recluse of Plas Gwyn?'

She smiled tremulously. 'It's you I have to thank for sending Mr Bergland to see me,' she said. 'I was afraid, before, but now I've decided to take a chance. Sammy is going to stay here with the Pritchards—she and Trefor are sweet on one another, anyhow—and I'm going to find out if I really am an actress.'

He stood up. 'You are, believe me,' he said. '"All's well that ends well"', then, to quote the Bard himself.'

Her heart seemed to swell as if it were about to burst with pain and anguish too great to be confined, too fierce for the facile relief of tears. How could all be well when he was about to walk out of her life again? How could it end well if she could not be close to him every day, could not see him, talk to him, hold him? She gazed at him with a flood of hopeless longing welling up inside her, unable to speak.

But that, so it would seem, was the way he wanted it. He had come to set all the records straight between them, to remove all misunderstanding, all acrimony, so that they could part friends, and that he had achieved. For him, that was enough, so there was nothing she could do but let him go in peace.

'Goodbye, Gareth,' she said, her voice little more than a whisper carried away by the breeze. She turned and began to walk up the path to the headland, dry-eyed, empty-hearted, every step a dragging weight as it carried her further and further away from all she desired.

*'Carenza!'*

The voice that could carry to the far corners of the largest auditorium without shouting reached her effortlessly. But Carenza could take no more. The more he prolonged this parting, the more it was bound to hurt her, and she was already hurting enough. She gasped and quickened her pace, then broke into a run, stumbling along the path, scarcely seeing where she was going, knowing only that she must get away before she broke into a million aching pieces.

He reached her just as she crested the headland and began the downward run. Seizing her by the shoulders, he spun her round to face him, and shook her.

'Don't run away from me, damn it! I won't allow it! Never run away from me again!' he said fiercely, and swept her up easily into his arms. Wild-eyed, she looked up into his face, and saw her own desperate intensity mirrored there for a split second, before his mouth came down on hers with ruthless sweetness.

Her resistance ended right there, she wound her arms around his neck and clung to him. Hers for one minute, an hour, or a lifetime, it was all the same.

'Carenza,' he said softly, urgently, as he at last released her mouth. 'I tried—I tried! You're young, and have all your life, your career in front of you, and I wanted to give it to you, free and clear. But I can't let you go!'

He drew her down on to the short, wind-cropped grass, rocking her in his arms, kissing her repeatedly.

'You told me once that you loved me,' he said. 'I told you it was all moonshine, and you said I was right.'

He gave a short laugh.

'Afterwards, I remembered those lines in *Othello* about the man who "threw a pearl away, richer than all his tribe." I knew too late that I loved you, but I truly thought that your life would be better without me.'

She had despaired of ever hearing him say those words to her, and now that he had she was so full to overflowing with emotions of joy, of relief, of incredulity that she could hardly find words to say to him in return. Her small hands cupped his face, and she covered it with quick kisses, her fingers tracing a pattern along the much-loved features, claiming them for her own.

'I don't want to be without you, Gareth,' she said at last. 'I've loved you since that day at Plas Gwyn, probably even before, although I was afraid to let myself admit it. But you weren't free of Celia, and

I thought there would never be a chance you would love *me*.'

'There's no chance, now, that I shall ever stop,' he told her seriously. 'When I love a woman, my darling, there are no half-measures. Perhaps that's why I, too, was afraid to get involved with you. But it happened all the same. I couldn't prevent it.'

He stood up, drawing her to her feet and holding her in the circle of his arms.

'Carenza, come back to Plas Gwyn with me, now,' he said urgently. 'I want to make love to you. I want to show you with more than words how much you mean to me. And you can be very sure that I won't ever let you go again.'

Her limbs grew weak at the very thought, and she clung tightly to him.

'Why, Mr Llewellyn!' she murmured happily. 'Are you proposing that we live in sin?'

'No, my sweet—this is Anglesey, not Hollywood, and I wouldn't dare outrage public opinion,' he chuckled. 'I'm planning on opening a bottle of champagne and asking you very properly to marry me, before taking you very improperly to bed!'

She smiled and held him even more closely, if that was possible.

'I'm glad you got them in the right order,' she said sternly, 'because I'm planning on saying yes to both propositions.'

For a long while they said nothing at all, because he was kissing her, and his kiss was telling her more than words ever could. Then he broke away, and looked down at her, with eyes suddenly authoritative and serious.

'I've no intention of blighting your career before it's got started, my love,' he said. 'How would you feel about making your debut as a junior member of the Shakespeare Trust?'

'I'd be ecstatic!' she gasped. 'There could be no better way to learn the craft—and I could be with you all the time.' She gave a wickedly impish grin. 'I don't expect to be your leading lady right away— but Marianne St John had better look to her laurels!'

His hand firmly under her chin, he lifted her face for his kiss once again.

'You'll always be the leading lady in my heart,' he promised. Closing her eyes with a sigh of content, she knew that was all she needed to hear.

# Mills & Boon

# Next month's Romances

Each month, you can choose from a world of variety in romance with Mills & Boon. These are the new titles to look out for next month.

**NO GENTLE SEDUCTION** Helen Bianchin

**THE FINAL TOUCH** Betty Neels

**TWIN TORMENT** Sally Wentworth

**JUNGLE ENCHANTMENT** Patricia Wilson

**DANCE FOR A STRANGER** Susanne McCarthy

**THE DARK SIDE OF DESIRE** Michelle Reid

**WITH STRINGS ATTACHED** Vanessa Grant

**BARRIER TO LOVE** Rosemary Hammond

**FAR FROM OVER** Valerie Parv

**HIJACKED HONEYMOON** Eleanor Rees

**DREAMS ARE FOR LIVING** Natalie Fox

**PLAYING BY THE RULES** Kathryn Ross

**ONCE A CHEAT** Jane Donnelly

**HEART IN FLAMES** Sally Cook

**KINGFISHER MORNING** Charlotte Lamb

*STARSIGN*

**STING IN THE TAIL** Annabel Murray

Available from Boots, Martins, John Menzies, W.H. Smith, Woolworths and other paperback stockists.

Also available from Mills and Boon Reader Service, P.O. Box 236, Thornton Road, Croydon, Surrey CR9 3RU.